ALL WE WANT
IS EVERYTHING

ALL WE WANT IS EVERYTHING

ANDREW F. SULLIVAN

ARP BOOKS · WINNIPEG

ARP Books (Arbeiter Ring Publishing)
201E-121 Osborne Street
Winnipeg, Manitoba
Canada R3L 1Y4
www.arpbooks.org

Printed in Canada by Kromar Printing
Cover by Michael Carroll
Cover image by Leigh Ledare
Typeset by Relish New Brand Experience

ARP acknowledges the financial support of our publishing activities by Manitoba Culture,
Heritage, and Tourism, and the Government of Canada through the Canada Book Fund.

ARP acknowledges the support of the Province of Manitoba through the Book Publishing
Tax Credit and the Book Publisher Marketing Assistance Program.

We acknowledge the support of the Canada Council for our publishing program.

With the generous support of the Manitoba Arts Council.

We would like to acknowledge funding support from the Ontario Arts Council, an agency
of the Government of Ontario.

Printed on paper with minimum 30% recycled post-consumer waste.

LIBRARY AND ARCHIVES CANADA CATALOGUING IN PUBLICATION

Sullivan, Andrew F., 1987-, author

　　All we want is everything / Andrew F. Sullivan.

Short stories.

ISBN 978-1-894037-84-6 (pbk.)

　　I. Title.

PS8637.U54A64 2013　　　C813'.6　　　C2013-901687-2

To Jen
Where all of this begins and ends.

Table of Contents

"We're not kings here; we're just strangers."
— Samuel T. Herring, "Vireo's Eye"

GOOD KING

BIG RED WAS ELBOW DEEP IN DEAD PIGEON WHEN HE HEARD THE crack like an ice-laden branch splitting from the trunk. He heard the shouts and the scream and that new kid with the ponytail, Barkwell, hollering over and over into the rafters. Big Red pulled his arms out of the heating duct and wiped the feathers and pigeon guts off on his Miami Heat T-shirt.

He'd stopped wearing good clothes to work after his manager, Kevin the Walrus, made him clean up a family of dead raccoons down in the receiving docks last September. Ruined his favourite shirt, the Harley Davidson one with the 1957 XL Sportster 883 on the front. His ex-wife had bought it for him down in North Carolina on their honeymoon. The little cubs had left a big yellow smear across the front. It was late December now. Pigeons had cooked alive when management decided to turn up the heat Monday morning. No one had bothered to trace the smell until Friday afternoon.

The younger temps yelled at each other as Big Red waddled down the deck. He spotted the glowing bald head of the Walrus hustling towards them across the liquor warehouse floor below, mouth buried into his shoulder mic. Red could see the crowd gathered around one of the hydraulic lifts, younger guys peering over the shoulders of the veterans.

One of the kids saw him walking towards them.

"Yo! Yo, Big Red! You see what one of your white boys tried to do? Yeah, the Segal motherfucker with the ponytail. He all up on Irwin like Irwin took his newspaper, like Irwin steals his shit all the time, right? Fuck man, Irwin don't even know Segal, you know? Irwin went wild with the bottle man, chucked it right at that ponytailed shit."

Another voice began spitting in Big Red's ear.

"Nah man, he took Segal's smokes and then just lied to his face like a bitch. Irwin always doin' shit like that just 'cause his Daddy drive a forklift on midnights."

Barkwell was lying on the floor with blood in his ponytail. Little Irwin nudged the body with a steel-toed boot. Hip-hop squeaked out over the concrete between them from a pair of bright red headphones. A shattered bottle of Gordon's lay diluting the blood dripping from Barkwell's ear.

Big Red pushed Irwin away and leaned down over the body. Barkwell probably weighed a hundred and twenty pounds. Big Red placed a bag of sawdust under the kid's small head. Barkwell's eyes stared up at the ceiling. Big Red breathed in deep, ready to apply mouth to mouth. Red was the only one on the shift with updated First Aid certification. His niece had almost drowned in the bathtub when he was babysitting her back in '97. He felt the kid's wrist, the pulse flitting in and out. He placed his lips on Barkwell's and the air filled his sinuses. Gin and copper and pine trees and pennies and a fork sticking out of his hand like a flag pole. The smell skipped into the receptors of his nose.

Christmas.

Barkwell smelled like Christmas.

The Christmas when Big Red and his two little cousins overdosed on Flintstones vitamins. A hazy blur of purple and orange puke all over the back of the living room sofa where they hid in wait for Santa. A string of pink and purple Wilmas and Dinos arranged on the window sill. Rations to help wait out Kris Kringle. The doctor in the emergency room warned Big Red's mother that the kids shouldn't eat any red meat for at least two weeks. He rubbed yellow fingers down her thigh and she asked him for a cigarette. Too much iron in those vitamins, he said and handed her a smoke. Big Red was only Little Red back then, but he still had a gut. The doctor patted his mother on the hip as they left and told her to watch the little porker's diet. Big Red watched her smile. The doctor waved goodbye through the glass of the emergency doors. His wide grin revealed a missing molar in the back of his mouth.

It was a Christmas when Grandma spilled gravy down her shirt and the dog tackled her into the Christmas tree. The same Christmas when Caleb Jackson smacked Big Red across the face so hard with his new baseball glove that Big Red saw stars. He sat on Caleb's face for five minutes until he heard him mumble Uncle, you fat stupid fat ass! Uncle! A Christmas when he got another status report from Mrs. Vandervlooten in the mail and a request for a parent-teacher conference. A Christmas when his cousins learned the words bitch and dick from Grandpa talking in his sleep. They watched *Raging Bull* and *Xanadu* on stolen cable in the living room.

Grandma was scrubbing the puke out from behind the couch when Dad finally arrived. He slid on the ice, holding a box of art supplies that Big Red suspected was his Christmas gift. A collection of water paints and charcoal sticks. Maybe some colouring books with Chinese subtitles. Christmas was supposed to have good presents. It wasn't like a birthday.

The year before, Dad had hung a fleet of preassembled and painted World War II planes from Big Red's ceiling. An epic dogfight stretched across the room for three months before Mom tore half of them down after she'd gone out one night with Aunt Shirley. Big Red stashed the remains of his fleet under the bed behind piles of Hardy Boys books and medical texts he'd lifted from Caleb Jackson's garage. Caleb's Dad said he didn't believe in doctors. You could teach yourself all that stuff if you put in the right amount of time and effort. Caleb's leg never healed right after he jumped off the roof playing Indiana Jones.

Birthdays. That was when Big Red's Dad always came up short. Over his last ten birthdays, Big Red had amassed three velvet paintings of his father, two badminton sets lifted from unsupervised backyards, one stuffed donkey with Kiss My Ass branded into the polyester and four sketches of his father's alternating cast of girlfriends drawn by Larry B., Dad's oldest, wisest friend. Larry B. still had three months left on his sentence before he'd be eligible for parole. Dad sent him some magazines for Christmas, but they never made it past the guards.

A Christmas when the Miami Heat finally won their second consecutive victory after a gruelling opening to their inaugural '88–'89 season that saw the team go 2–20 before Boxing Day. Always supportive of the underdog, Big Red's Dad walked across the icy driveway decked out head to toe in Heat gear. He had a ball cap on his head with all the tags still attached.

"I heard you chewed up Bedrock last night, little man!"

A Christmas when Big Red sat at the dinner table as his father tried to explain the will and grit he attributed to players like Kevin Edwards, Rory Sparrow and Rony Seikaly. About overcoming the adversity they saw on the court and how they were always willing to press on despite devastating losses. A Christmas when Uncle Rod cautioned Big Red's Dad about mixing wine and gin together and Big Red covered his ears as his Grandma started belting out Christmas carols to announce the food was ready. His two little cousins did the same.

"Get your hands off your ears, kids! Grandma likes everyone to hear her singing."

After failing at running an auto shop, a catalogue sales business, and eventually losing his fishing boat to the tax authorities, Big Red's father had a lot in common with the Miami Heat. For Big Red's last birthday, his father and Larry B. took him to Red Lobster. They made him try everything gross on the menu before dine-and-dashing. Oysters. Crab legs. Scallops like rubber stamps. Larry fell and got caught in between the double doors after Big Red pushed them the wrong way. The police arrested Larry, claiming he'd broken his parole. Big Red's Dad got so mad he left Red downtown for five hours. Grandma finally found him outside the Genosha Hotel, watching the men in big coats sneak out the back door with women in tall shoes.

A Christmas when his father's plates were from the States and a new girl's photo dangled from the rear-view mirror. She was covered in sand. Just like the Heat, Big Red's father was often on the road, delivering water and air purifiers for one of those infomercial guys with the fake hair and smooth orange skin. The ones Big Red saw on TV when he stayed up late at Caleb's house. Sleep is for the weak, Caleb's Dad would say. He drank twenty-five cups of coffee a day. Big Red counted the mugs stacked around the desk in the basement. Caleb's Dad didn't like to keep clocks in the house.

Big Red watched as his grandmother set the dishes down on the three tables his mother had pushed together in the dining room to make one long, haphazard peninsula she could disguise with white tablecloths. Splotches of cranberry stains from another Christmas stood out in faded halos on the underside of the sheet. Big Red's mother hadn't applied the cold water in time, and she was afraid of bleach.

"I think my favourite player has to be Pearl. Oh come on, you don't know Dwayne fucking 'Pearl' Washington? First round pick in '86? Looks tiny out there, 'cause he's only like 6'2". But he's so quick, so good… he's definitely a core part of the team. He drives for it even when you can see the others are slacking. Even if they're down by twenty points in the last quarter and no one else seems to care, Pearl's working like they only need one more shot to seal the deal and net another win… you know like a real champion. Like a black Larry Bird, but like shorter and you know… curly hair…"

A Christmas when Big Red's father stopped taking his lithium. A month earlier his girlfriend's brother raised all these health concerns at a kegger outside of Tampa. Muscle damage, bone loss, hypertension and early onset adult diabetes. Her brother was a diabetic selling his needles for two dollars a pop at this kegger. Health, man, he said, revealing a mouth of gold fillings. It's the only thing you've got in the end. Big Red's father nodded. He off-loaded the prescriptions on the brother for forty dollars apiece. Enough money to buy his son a good Christmas present. Make up for that whole birthday thing when he forgot Big Red downtown and the cops put Larry B. away for another six months.

"He's going to be with that team a hell of a long time man, put-ting up the numbers like he is. Oh I know he doesn't look like it. Funny they look so short on TV right, 'cause they'd be like fucking giants if they came in here right now, you know? I wish I'd seen him like playing for Syracuse, or even the Nets... well obviously the Nets 'cause Jersey needs a power forward... and yeah I know he's small, but like... he could... like change the whole nature of the game... play on a brand new level... shit, you know what I'm saying Rod? Let me top you off there, alright?"

A Christmas when Big Red would reach for a dinner roll while his Grandma sang "Good King Wenceslas" and laid the sweet potato pie out on the table in front of his mother. The same Christmas when his father would seize his fork and jam it deep through his eleven-year-old son's hand into the soft top of the card table under the tablecloth, grinning at Uncle Rod over a glass of wine spiked with gin. A Christmas when everyone started screaming and his cousins were crying and the living room still smelled like puked up Barney Rubble and the dog knocked over the Christmas tree three times during the afternoon. Grandma kept shrilly singing, "When the snow lay round about, deep and crisp and even!"

"Wait for Grandma to say grace, Red. You're getting too big for your belly."

The ambulance that took Big Red to the hospital decided to stop at every red light along the way. He stared at the four metal prongs glowing like alien bones in his flesh. The same yellow-fingered doctor from the night before asked him who did this and was he the same one who made him eat all those vitamins last night? This was a Christmas when Children's Aid asked Big Red a series of questions in the hospital bed while his mother stood outside the room, running her hand through the doctor's hair, ignoring the missing molar, the yellow fingers and the high pitched laugh because she had a mortgage three months in arrears. A wide lady with too much makeup quizzed Big Red about his father and about his school and about the time his grandfather left him at Tim Horton's in Sault Ste. Marie after a fishing trip and his mother had called the police.

A Christmas when Big Red forgot his Ghostbusters in a snow bank and his father got arrested for the third time in as many years. The following June his Dad would plead out to institutional observation for a period of no less than three months. Around the same week, Dwayne "Pearl" Washington would finally receive his release from the Miami Heat after fifty-four games, never to play in the NBA again. This was a Christmas when Big Red finally got his report card from Mrs. Vandervlooten. He had been answering all the math questions with drawings of animals—a lot of ducks and pandas. She said she was concerned, very concerned with his performance. This was a Christmas when Big Red realized "concerned" didn't mean much at all as a nurse eased the fork out of his hand.

Walrus stared at Big Red. His moustache was damp with sweat. The warehouse was almost empty now, forklifts pulling into their parking spots on the floor to recharge for the day shift. The chill outside still made the whole place damp and Big Red felt the day's sweat cooling all over his back and along the creases of his skin.

"I want this cleaned up in the next twenty minutes before the guys from Labour get here, alright? The puddle makes it look worse than it is. Nobody died here. The kid is going to be fine.

I mean the one that got hit, not that other fuck with the glasses. They already picked him up in a car with cuffs. He's not our problem anymore. But the puddle needs to go. Now."

Walrus handed Big Red a mop wet end first.

"And Red? Next time you want to make out with a boy, do it on your own time, alright? If I want, I can watch that shit at home on the Internet. I swear you just about passed out on that kid and suffocated him with those tits of yours. Smothered him with your endless love. Ha, you like that? You wanna be Big Love or Endless Love? That'll be good. I'll let you choose. I say go with Big Love; it suits you best. Don't worry; you'll get time-and-a-half for the OT tonight. All fifteen minutes of it. Get it done before the lights go out."

Walrus walked away, shaking his bald head. Red stirred the grey water in the bucket beside him. He spotted a fly trying to crawl out of the muck and pushed it back down with the mop. The warehouse floor was tacky with blood and gin. The sawdust made it stick even worse. Under his breath, Big Red began to hum Christmas carols. His old T-shirt was still dotted with pigeon guts and now spackled with Barkwell's blood too. He kept mopping.

After a while, Big Red went to change the water.

CROWS EAT WELL

THE DAY I GET OUT ON PAROLE, TOBY PICKS ME UP IN KINGSTON. HE'S two hours late.

"You got skinny, brother. Big boys steal your food in there? Call it the lock-up diet?"

The sky is empty above us as we hit the outskirts of town. Toby's got all the windows open, but the car still smells like bud and Burger King wrappers. The radio dial is covered in grease.

"We gotta go check in on the old man; he's been after Mom again. Dropped a full ton of gravel in her driveway last week. Said since she kept the rock on her finger, he may as well add to the pile. Spray painted happy birthday over the whole thing, too. Asshole still remembers her birthday out of spite, I swear to God. And she won't shut up about it. He's still got it in for you, by the way, so maybe you can talk it out. Just don't get me too involved, okay?"

Up and down both sides of the highway, sunflowers stand hunched over brittle stalks. Their massive heads droop down toward the poisoned soil. Too much fertilizer makes it impossible for them to follow the sun. A few ruptured husks blow onto the road, but the tires crush them as we drive past. Crows circle above the yellow rows in silence.

"I shoulda probably got you some new clothes or let you shower, eh?" Toby says, but he has no intention of pulling over. "You smell like that pink soap they got in movie theatre shitters."

It was my idea to try and steal the bulldozer three years ago. I knew how to get under the fences on Dad's property, knew where he kept the keys and the combinations. I knew that there were always guys in need of a bulldozer—my logic was fuzzy at the time, interspersed with ten-hour binges in the dark where I believed all my dreams could come to life along the dirty edge of a windowsill, all within my reach. Oxy does that sometimes—it lets you believe. Stealing a bulldozer did not seem out of reach. I could still drive standard even though my license was suspended. My only problem was outrunning the cops once I drove into a ditch.

I don't blame Kali for it. We were both cooped up in that basement apartment, breathing in each other's fumes, rubbing powder on our gums and trying to say I love you through gritted teeth. The word forever occasionally slipped out too, before we started to grind our jaws into dust. I watched my legs slowly deteriorate under the quilts, the muscles from cross-country withering after months without use that winter. Mom blamed Dad for the backhoe running over my foot in high school, but I still tried to run afterward. The pain pills helped me keep up. They made everything lighter around the edges. I barely noticed the downward incline at first.

"I tried calling Dad before I grabbed you. Apparently the newspaper people came by, wanted to interview him. All the neighbours are out front at Mom's, taking pictures of the gravel pile. She tried shovelling it this morning, but gave up after a while. Half the letters are still there, but I don't think it says happy birthday anymore. Maybe just 'hap.' Something like that."

While I was in the hospital in high school, Mom egged Dad's truck twice before demanding a divorce. He rear-ended her car in the long-term parking and keyed the entire left side during one of my physio treatments. The signed court papers were tucked under the wipers. I told him to go home, go find a new home and get the fuck out, so he bought a farm outside of town and stopped calling. That's where he kept all the equipment for excavating. I stopped working for him in the summers, tired of accidentally digging up dead dogs and septic tanks in the heat.

Toby likes to call my accident the catalyst, but he failed Grade 10 chemistry so I don't give much weight to what he says. These things take time—nothing is instant. I don't believe in stars or signs or all that horoscope shit. Stuff happens. I'm a Rabbit according to the Chinese, but Kali might have been lying about that. I'm not that fast anymore and most of my nerves are shot.

"Almost there," Toby says. "Now if he says anything about you smelling like shit, you can just blame that on me. I know I haven't been the best of brothers or anything. He's almost forgiven me for growing weed in the back fields, so I'll take the hit for you this time."

The car comes over a crest and I see a figure out in the fields, walking toward the house. There are no sunflowers out here. Just rows and rows of corn and lonely scarecrows emerging like stop signs every fifty feet to scare off all the birds. They don't pay much attention.

"I'm sure it'll be no hard feelings or anything," Toby says. "You still talkin' to Kali? I seen her around a bit, but I think she was a little too interested in me, so I kept my distance. Don't want to ruin a good thing. Thought you might appreciate that, right?"

"Sure do, buddy. Sure," I say. Toby moved in with Dad after everything went down in the divorce. I was already eighteen, so I just let it be. Mom would call me and ask for help in the garden, and I'd show up once in a while. I'd try running around the backyard, kicking up my heels to feel the tendon in my right foot twang. The doctors prescribed more meds and I started working in the hospital cafeteria. No one there asked me if I would be running any more 10ks.

"You might even see her out there, actually. I seen her walking around town a lot."

I met Kali while in rehab for my foot. She was in Toby's grade, but school never interested her much after her step-Dad broke her hand in the car door one April. Her Mom ended up requiring a restraining order, but Kali said she saw him sometimes outside her bedroom window at night, asking for forgiveness. He was never dressed for the weather and always dripping wet.

Kali couldn't write with her left, so all her notes slopped to one side across the page. Sometimes her words slurred out between her lips as well, but I don't think it was related to the hand. She told me the boys at school called her Strokes before she asked to borrow my medication while we smoked outside the visitor doors with the old men in wheelchairs and nurses on break. I never asked Toby about it—I never knew about his bullshit crush. He was the one who spotted me in the middle of the night driving the bull-dozer through the gate three years ago. He didn't call the cops—just told Dad about it.

"Well, let's go lay down some rules. You know for the last three years I had to play peacekeeper while you were all cozy watching TV in your cell? They are like dogs in a pit, man. Tearing each other's ears off and shit. I've seen it happen—with the dogs, I mean. I wouldn't put it past Mom though. She still sends lilies on his birth-day, you know, like for a funeral? Get outta the car and we'll talk to him. I live with the asshole and he barely speaks to me."

The wind tears at my clothes when I stand up. The first few months in jail were full of withdrawal—the puking and the sweats. I watched my fingernails grow and my beard wrap itself around my face. There was too much effort involved in maintenance. My crotch became a bush that I didn't even bother to examine after a while. Everything was too tangled.

"He still digging holes like there's something to find?" I ask.

"Always, buddy. Always."

Toby and I walk toward the fields. The sun is directly above us. There are no shadows following us out here. I kick at the gopher holes and try to avoid ants swarming around my feet.

"So they let him go, eh? And he didn't even bring a boyfriend."

Dad's teeth are bright yellow. He's got a cigarette tucked in one corner of his mouth, but it doesn't seem to obstruct his words. There's a red ball cap on his head covered in salt rings. Toby starts plucking at ears of dead corn, dropping kernels onto the ground. On closer inspection, all the plants in here are just like the sunflowers. Something in the soil has accelerated all this growth; everything is overripe and slowly bursting.

"You know you could have called me first, son. And Toby, I don't wanna hear nothing about your Mom. She can deal with that mess on her own. I didn't even say much to the papers anyway. It'll all blow over eventually. She still sends me black cards on Valentine's."

"You're like children," I start to say. "Like the world is a sandbox or some shit to you."

I can feel sweat running down my spine. I remember Dad in the courtroom, explaining how much the 'dozer was worth, how it was totalled. Detailing my past substance abuse issues, as he called them, my learning problems as a child and my mother's overprotective nature. I heard him yelling at Kali outside the courtroom, mocking the way her voice slurred in stressful moments. He asked if she charged men by the hour. I was convicted of attempted robbery and resisting arrest. The bulldozer was considered a dangerous weapon.

"Look, you and your brother may think you know a lot of things. I never tried to play easy with you. Always gave you room to make mistakes. Just tried to balance out your mother. The world ain't ever fair like she expects. Sometimes the world shits on you."

There are crows around us in the field, picking at the corn. Nothing is too rotten here. There are still pieces they can salvage. Even now, the crows can eat well.

Kali would stop in from time to time on visitor days. She'd pass me notes about the program they had her in, the shelter that was protecting her from the elements and the groping hands of whoever found her in the dark. She still woke up sometimes with her step-Dad's face laughing in the rain, but there were no windows in her room. The visits began to slow down after a while. Mom told me Kali wasn't showing up at the house much anymore. Sometimes she'd see her standing on a corner, smoke rising above her head, her legs torn and ragged at the knees. I practiced punching the wall in my cell and writing down the facts about each run I'd made before they locked me up. I tried to pinpoint the smells and the way mud stuck to my shoes. I tracked every leaf lying in my path and remembered the pain inside my shins, the fissures in my tendons, the ache of my lungs when all I could breathe out was steam—I wanted it back.

"Mom just wants you to pick the stones back up, Dad," Toby says. "Give me the keys to the truck and I'll go do it. She said she's going to call the cops…"

"And what did I do that was illegal exactly? You want to ask your brother about that? I don't think I broke any laws. He is the expert after all. Got a three-year education, if I remember it correctly. They can investigate if they want, but if you ask me, it sounds like your mother is just looking her gift horse in the mouth. She got a brand new driveway in the deal!"

Eventually, I didn't want Kali to come back. I didn't want to be reminded of floating in that basement apartment, my synapses firing in all the wrong directions to bolster fantasies I couldn't even name. Rabbits and all the spirit animals I denied, all the constellations forming over and over again across the network of my skull in the shape of bulldozers and excavators backing over my foot while laughing at the scream. I was focused on the pain instead, the one that rattled through my stupid foot and the old lungs I remembered, the ones that could taste the cold.

"Dad, you remember what she said after the excavator? You remember all that shit?"

His eyes shrink down to slits under the sun. He's always wearing that stupid hat.

"What about it? You shouldn't have been standing there in the first place, I told you that a hundred times and I told your mother too, but she just doesn't listen, you know that."

I take a step towards him, avoiding the holes in the rotten soil around us.

"I agree. I should have been more careful. Coulda been a lot different if I had, but I didn't. And that's my mistake. Shouldn't have taken that 'dozer either, no shit, that's for sure."

"No shit, indeed," he says and tries to back away. Toby keeps picking at the corn.

"But you know what Mom said about all of that? Before she started egging your trucks and mailing flowers, and all that stupid shit? It was stupid, I can't deny that. She said, you know what, your father makes a living scavenging other's mistakes, digging up their shit..."

"Now son, you better watch what you're saying. First day of parole and all, right? You don't want to do anything that might send you back into a place like that."

Six months before my planned release, Kali finally came in to see me again. I had some bug racking my body. My eyes were pink and hazy, but I could see the bruises around her neck, the wounds trickling up the insides of her arms like warnings for something else, and I didn't want to see it. I didn't have to anyway. She told me all about the nights out in the cold, the fits of scratching and the tastes of all those things inside her mouth. She told me about him picking her up one night, his eyes hidden beneath the brim of a ball cap, and that he didn't ask for anything. He just wanted to remind her of what she was and what she'd done to all of us. She was just another piece of shit he pulled up to the surface. He drove her fifteen miles outside town and then told her to get out. He told her to walk and watch out for cars. They might think they just hit an animal and keep on driving; they might not even notice the crunch of bone out there in the dark.

I didn't want to hear anymore. I ran. And ran. I ran into the wall and the wall again. My head was bleeding when the guards tackled me to the floor. They pushed me down onto the tiles and slapped six more months onto my wait. I didn't do much for a while after that.

"I don't really give a shit about parole, I just wanna tell you what Mom said while you were busy keying her car in the parking lot. A living of digging up other people's shit, she said, because you can't bear to look at your own. Now does that sound about right? Too much time trolling through everyone else's garbage, yeah? What do you have buried out here anyway?"

Dad takes a step back, but the dirt can't hold him. It collapses around his right leg and he plunges into the wet, damp soil. I yank his hat off his head and toss it into the corn.

"You still listen to that bu-bitch?" he stutters. "Still a momma's boy like before."

Toby stands behind us without moving. He has nothing to say anymore. I do smell like public bathroom soap. Dad tries to pull himself out of the ground, tearing at the soil around him. I spit down onto the shining bald head below me and kick him in the teeth once. They make a snapping sound and then my bad foot is wet. I don't need to do it again.

"Toby, you gotta go call someone," he coughs. There are jagged bits of bone and blood where his mouth was, but he doesn't cry out. "Just get back to the goddamn house!"

I turn, but Toby is already fleeing through the corn. Crows erupt behind him like a plague.

I used to run like that. You should have seen me.

PUMPKINHEADS

THE COMPANY DOES NOT SEND FLOWERS.

Anita receives condolences from her neighbours and old high
school friends. Bouquets arrive from across the country, from family members stranded down in Texas and a great aunt who writes
from somewhere in southern Oregon. They tell her to call and
to write, to spread the grief around, maybe dilute it along phone
lines or in emails from Juan's old account. Anita can't remember
the password. It had something to do with the ugly dog that Juan
tried to buy off his brother—Hercules. A stupid name for a dog,
Anita told him. A stupid name for anyone, really.

There are cards from her step-sisters and the kid who cuts
the lawn. One of her old high school boyfriends sent a postcard
with his cell phone number on the back. Bright pink letters fill
the living room and some of the plants are already beginning to
rot. The kids crunch dead petals under their feet and the cat tries
to eat the tiny pieces they leave behind. It pukes in the corners of
her bedroom and no one bothers to clean it up. The house is full
of apologies and longwinded poems about grief and forgiveness.
They all use the word *time* like it means something when your husband has been broken into three pieces. They use words like *destiny*
and *recovery*. Anita runs flower stems down the garbage disposal.

She crushes tulips and roses into potpourri. She stops counting the letters and tries to sleep. She wakes up to doorbells and phone calls and the ever-ringing sound of her alarm clock trapped under Juan's old work clothes.

The company does not send flowers though. The company just bills her for the ambulance.

Anita sits in the coffee shop across from the foundry. Her hair is up, showing off the ears Juan liked to kiss when he thought she was asleep. She didn't want to ruin the illusion, so she had always remained still. She has cut most of her hair off now. It lies somewhere in a drain under the city, waiting to join a larger mass of cast-off things. Anita has burned most of Juan's clothes behind the house. The neighbours balked, but did not call the police. They just watched the smoke rise and whispered back and forth about her children. There are no play-dates.

"There's a new batch every day it seems."

The man across from her points to the line of men outside the foundry. They wear bright orange hard hats and smoke cigarettes right down to the filter. Some have bracelets around their right ankles. Others massage scars from burns that run like furrows down their chests. Serpents and tigers clash with the many faces of the Virgin Mary on their hairy forearms.

"Place just grinds through them, but that's what you gotta do. Keep bringing in new blood. Another batch of pumpkinheads. They got no idea what they are in for, of course. Wouldn't be able to get them this cheap if they did."

The man across from Anita knew her husband. He worked on the same shift, sitting in an office above the main floor. He watched the numbers, trying to boost productivity. He was the one who called toilet paper and soap luxuries, the one who suggested employees bring their own supplies. His name is George Allison and he was the one who found Juan underneath the conveyor belt. He was the only one who insisted they call an ambulance before cleaning up the scene. He was the one who snatched the bone fragments off the floor and covered it in bleach.

"Now Juan, he was no pumpkinhead. Ten years working on pipe doesn't make you stupid. He was just unlucky in a place like that. And I woulda taken care of him, you know that, right? If the doctors hadn't fucked it up, he might have still been with us today."

George Allison called a few weeks after the funeral. He told her about what he saw, and how the company hadn't done Juan right by his standards. There were still kids to be fed and that house wasn't paying for itself. George offered to meet her for coffee. He offered to provide a helping hand. He was single and he was tired of living alone in his apartment. All his fish kept dying. He could never get the balance right. The chemicals never hit an equilibrium. Eventually, he just filled the aquarium with coloured sand and forgot about it. All the fish went down the toilet with everything else George Allison couldn't stomach. His fridge was filled with yogurt.

"And now I realize this might be a little forward, you know, it isn't easy for me to ask like this," George says. He runs his soft hands through some spilled sugar on the table. His hands are pink and white and they shake a bit when he tries to speak. They look like baby birds. "But I was wondering if you might want to, uhm, well go on out and get some food with me or something? Not a lunch like this, but something that adults might do. Something to get your mind off the kids and everything else. You know if you feel like it."

Anita does not say much. She flicks some sugar onto the floor with her thin fingers. Her eyes stare out at the pumpkinheads across the street, collected from the prisons and halfway houses out here in the country. She wants to warn them, but she has never been inside the plant. She only heard stories from Juan about massive gouts of molten iron pouring across the floor and an industrial oven that once exploded in the basement. Two of his friends ended up in the hospital. Anita looks at George Allison and all she sees is some limp bird flopping toward her.

"I guess we could do something. I'll have to find someone to watch the kids."

George's face breaks out into a nervous grin. His lips can't hide his teeth.

"Whatever you need, to uhm, do, you just get it done. I will pick you up. Sorry that we had to meet at a place like this—I just can't leave the plant for too long, as you know."

His hands flutter up off the table for a few seconds. He moves in to kiss her cheek, but it somehow lands on her ear. Only then does Anita realize his nose feels like a beak.

By the third time they sleep together, George has already begun to move his stuff into the house. The closet is filled with his shirts and there are boxes of books about the future of economic development and the colonization of Mars fifteen centuries from now. In George's world, it seems everything is possible. Cars will only get bigger, phones will only get smaller. There is so little out of our reach. We just need to focus. This is what he tells Anita as they lie in bed and talk about the future. They talk about a bigger house and three cars and investing in educations for Paul and Anna. The children still call him George and the cat will not sit on his lap, but George is a patient man. He keeps track of how much toilet paper everyone uses and rarely adds salt to any of his meals. Anita's friends say he is a catch and the neighbours stop asking about the pile of burnt clothes in the backyard. George has those removed discreetly.

It has only been a month or two, but George tells Anita she has nothing to worry about. She runs one hand down his chest, searching for hair she can't find. His whole body is pink and it sweats in tiny bursts in the middle of the night. The sheets are wet with perspiration and everything smells damp when they wake up in the morning. Anita asks him what happened when he found Juan underneath the conveyor belt. George tries to grab her breast, and she pushes away his hand. He usually climbs on top and watches her eyes when they make love. He calls it making love and Anita lets him because she does not believe he ever learned to fuck.

"You really want to know? I mean, it was not pleasant. Some of the guys had to take a step back. He had probably been down there for a while. It's hard to hear someone over the sound of all those machines. We had the health and safety guys tell us something about jet engines, but they never really gave us any guidelines to improve upon the safety measures."

"What was he doing when you found him?" Anita asks. She's cut her hair back even further. Her ears are fully exposed in the dark and she can hear every wet word George spits out into the darkness. She wants to know why he sweats so much, but she knows he won't respond well to questions like that. He doesn't like to be asked about his family or the way he uses a fork—like it's a shovel or a piece of heavy machinery. Anita asks him about the foundry instead. She asks him about the injuries, the burns and the ever-rotating cast of pumpkinheads—lambs in a lion's den, according to George. They are chaff on the floor. They are all replaceable. He hires and fires, but he doesn't really make too many decisions. Those come from somewhere in Alabama, behind a desk larger than his car. He is just an instrument, he tells her. A powerful one, but useless in the wrong hands. His little bird hands jump across her body in the dark, describing workers with duct tape wrapped around their hands after the cloth gloves fail in the foundry. She insists he tell her about Juan, and his hands retreat under the sheets.

"He was… well, he was still awake when we found him. The shirt he was wearing, it was too loose for maintenance work. Old Juan wasn't really thinking that one through, you know? We always wanna promote safety down there, but a minute down is a minute lost. Three fittings going a minute—we start to fall behind if the system gets shutdown. So Juan went down there when the conveyor was still running. And the guard, well, the guards can cause a lot of extra jams. They call them 'safety' guards, but all they really do is gum up the works. It's like taking a craftsman's hands and putting them in rubber gloves. It doesn't help anyone."

Anita stares at the ceiling fan above her. She watches its blade rotate and remembers what Juan looked like at the hospital. His left arm was a nub, worn down by the spinning wheels and the relentless pressure of the conveyor belt. Its rollers had broken the bones inside his hand. The top of his head was chipped and the scalp was split like some rotten peel, leaking out all kinds of fluid onto the sheets as the doctors fought with the body to contain its liquid life. His mouth hung open, but chunks of his cheek had been worn away. Half his face looked back at her, but the pain made it distant, unfounded. Juan was somewhere in a haze and he could only grasp at the air with his right hand. It was undamaged. His wedding band was gone, swallowed up somewhere by that machine. Anita never bothered to ask for someone to find it down there in the greasy darkness.

"I was one of the first ones who heard him, and by then most of his arm was gone. He was still screaming, but the thing... look, Anita, I don't need to tell you the rest of this, do I? I mean this is something that won't ever be happening again, you know? Like, we have a plan now."

Anita shakes her head. She wants him to continue. The air is filled with their sweat and the fan keeps tossing it up against the windows in waves of condensation. She wraps her hands around the bed frame's bars and asks George to continue.

"Well, most of his arm was gone. And he wasn't really talking, more like, just heaving around. It smelled pretty bad, it was like a grinder or something, you know? He didn't even recognize me. I was the one who had them shut down the machine and I made damn sure there was an ambulance coming. I pulled him out and he was looking at me, but the thing had already ripped out so much of his hair. And he was bleeding all over the place, so I had to go and get something to start cleaning it up. I mean, it was just too much. No one was going to understand that. I mean the system runs and when we need to fix it, we have to do with what we have..."

Anita nods and tells him she understands. Her children seem to like George well enough. All his books are organized and he even irons her clothes. He can't cook, but he does try and clean the dishes. The heavy water leaves his hands wrinkled and spent. He still works at the foundry for fifty hours a week, calling her on his lunch breaks to talk about the latest pumpkinhead disaster. They have applied new policies since Juan's death, but no one has launched an investigation. The conveyor belt that swallowed up Juan's arm is still alive, still moving in perpetual stasis without a thought of remorse or failure. It is just cogs and rollers and an endless pull toward a goal it can't ever reach. It is never satisfied. It only wants more.

In the darkness, Anita can feel George growing hard against her leg. She ignores the sensation and tries to pretend she is asleep. Somewhere in the wet air of their old bedroom, Juan asks her to hold his hand. The smooth nub he points in her direction drips all over the sheets.

George proposes once all the flowers are dead and gone. He makes sure all the letters from relatives and family friends are packed up into boxes and hidden in the basement. The company's requests and payment statements are shredded and burned in the oven. George fills the bookshelves with textbooks and the collected works of Isaac Asimov. All of it's alphabetical.

Everything is balanced. Even the new couch is centred in the living room, perfectly situated under the bay window. Anita still keeps all the blinds closed, but the neighbours say the children are behaving better. They do not cry out in the middle of the night and they have stopped capturing the local cats in homemade cages. George teaches them how to multiply and he even designs a chore chart for the bathroom on the first floor. Paul and Anna take turns scrubbing the toilet bowl. They learn long division and begin to memorize all fifty states without pausing.

Anita is standing over the sink with the dishes. They've had lasagne again. Pieces of it float up above the soap like crusty bits of skin. George likes to have lasagne after a hard day dealing with the regulators. They've been by a lot more recently, asking questions about the forklifts and their braking systems. Another pumpkinhead lost his helmet when one of the trucks backed up too quickly in the loading bay. The files all land on George's desk, where his hands flit from folder to folder, repurposing burns and cuts as minor injuries and reworking doctor's orders to result in light duty for injured employees who clean the toilets and unpack cleaning supplies. They are known as the malingerers by management and they are all missing pieces. Some of them bear burns along their forearms and others have fingers mashed into thick wads of paste.

"The problem is the guidelines are so vague. What constitutes a violation? Well, you can't ask me. They hire me on to hire these guys, and now I am stuck watching out for fire hazards and dust floating in the air. Dust? Now dust is killing guys? You have to wonder what they are going to think of next, Anita. They really can't expect us to follow every new trend. If we believe everything in those journals, well then, everything is killing us. May as well blame the stars for shining and the water for running. Eventually it will wear down the rocks. Just what happens. People break down. The world doesn't stop. We don't either."

The kids are outside throwing weeds at each other. Dandelions keep sprouting up no matter how much pesticide George puts down on the lawn. Anita is thinking about Juan's old wedding band lying under the dust and the grease on the pit floor. The conveyor belt must have spat it out somewhere into the dark. Her own rings hide in the bathroom cabinet. They've been replaced by a new stone from George, one that seems to consume her finger. Even on cloudy days, it spits out rays of bright light. She has already scratched the car with it twice. It sits on the edge of the sink and watches her as another dish emerges, still scabbed with burnt cheese. A wave of dirty water with chunks of pasta pulls the ring down into the sink and Anita tries not to laugh.

"It fell into the sink again, George."

"Annie, you really need to keep an eye on that thing. I can't be buying it again."

She steps away as George stalks over to the sink. Both kids pelt each other with dead dandelions outside. Yellow streaks cover their cheeks. Anita watches them shouting, but the glass keeps out the noise. They are sealed away. No one can hear a thing they say.

"Now you gotta remember to leave it in a glass or something when you're doing the dishes. Once it's gone, it's gone. You think I'm breaking the bank again, you got another thing coming."

George's hands search for the ring, scraping their way across the bottom of the sink. They investigate the utensils and the bits of food clinging to the edges. He finally finds the stone circling the drain, rattling against the pipe, almost plunging beyond his reach. His tiny bird hands clutch at the ring and fight to pull it out of the hole. They are bright pink in the hot water.

"I found the littler bugger—"

Anita presses her hand against the disposal button and listens to him shriek. The kids outside continue throwing weeds at each other. George screams again, but Anita leaves her hand on the button. The machine gurgles and coughs up red, choppy water onto the kitchen floor. She presses the button down again and listens to it churning. She listens to George shrieking.

She wonders if Juan sounded any different.

THE MAGICIAN RIDES AGAIN

SO WE FIND HIM OUT IN BARRIE, HIS HEAD HANGING DOWN BETWEEN scabbed knees. Floor covered in puke, the McDonald's fries still holding their shape and consistency amongst the orange sludge, except they're white like bones and for a minute we think maybe the Magician ate a mouse whole or something. Maybe he swallowed a bird or ate a pigeon. We think this because we've seen him jump off the roof of a two-story semi-detached onto a child's trampoline and also watched him pee off an overpass into oncoming traffic in broad daylight. But in the end, it is just fries and all of a sudden no one is hungry. The Magician is rocking back and forth on the floor covered in these white fries and telling the two of us to go away, go the fuck away. His face is covered in dirt and there are fresh marks on his arms oozing something thick and yellow and wrong. He points a finger in the air and the blood blisters glow bright pink under the light.

The Magician has no tricks. He can't pick a card, any card, can't guess your age; he can't even pull a bouquet of roses out of his vest. He has no vest, just old cargo shorts and a T-shirt that says WOODBINE RACETRACK: FOR THE HORSE PEOPLE OF ONTARIO. He has no secret rabbit, no top hat, no amazing feats of illusion or mystery to torment inquiring minds. The Magician is the Magician because of his moustache, a long tendril of patchy fur stretching straight across his upper lip and extending two inches outward onto each pock-marked cheek like worn upholstery. The Magician has no sleeve full of kerchiefs and no assistant to distract the crowd. He only has twenty-two teeth left and he keeps repeating his old postal code like a beacon signal. We try to pick him up off the floor and he shakes us off before stumbling into an iron bed frame across the room. He spits out something green and mumbles that it's our fault, all our fault, and no one tells him he's wrong.

Even after forty-three days stumbling through the province in some kind of pharmacy-fuelled haze, the Magician's moustache remains stable and unyielding to the stubble on his face. It stands out against the dirt and flaking skin. It is the one trait we can rely on to find him when he disappears, when he ducks out at work or ditches his apartment. Dead fish and plants remain behind like damp ashes. Landlords call to declare him as an evicted tenant; supervisors announce his immediate termination in letters we receive in the mail. The Magician does not care. He floats along the cloverleaves of highways and lingers in truck stops between London and Woodstock, waiting for a ride, a hit, another rise before the coming fall, because there's always a fall. The Magician can't outrun it and Uncle Albert has stopped paying for the rehab and the rental units and the fines for public urination, destruction of public property and the ever-recurring ghost of indecent exposure.

Me and Carl got him in at the warehouse slugging booze and unloading trucks. We spent two hours convincing the night shift manager those snakes tattoos wrapped around the Magician's stringy forearms were from the army, rewards for blowing up some sand people or whatever lie the manager wanted to hear that night. Night shift managers always own too many guns—always see too much roadkill on their commute home in the morning after everyone has gone to sleep. They clean up after the rest of us and so their world is made up of concentrated disinfectant mixtures, heavy curtains and endlessly detailed over-time sheets.

The Magician lasted two weeks riding the bus, eating ham sandwiches and flossing his teeth during the commute. He told everyone about his days riding horses, the pure thoroughbreds on Uncle Albert's farm. No one was listening. We sat at a different table to avoid all the shit they threw his way. He tried to tell them about the farm up north of the city, how the grass smelled, what fresh milk tasted like when he was a kid. They all called him the Mexican Pedo behind his back. We tried to get them to change it to the Magician, tried to explain we were his cousins, but nicknames stick worse than ticks once you stepped inside. Mexi Ped came next and after that Maxi Pad followed in its course. They left tampons in his locker and stuffed a few in his lunch bag on breaks. When the caf served tomato soup, the Magician would find it splashed all down his line, gumming up the works, lingering for days like a dead mouse between the rollers.

He tried to tell them about the one race up in Sudbury, the one where Uncle Al left him down at the hotel bar the night before, the one where he slid off the horse and got his face trampled by That Ghost Just Ain't Holy Anymore, Juniper, and The Last True Austrian. Their collective hooves rearranged his face and Uncle Al's number one stallion, Charles Bronson iii, broke a leg in two places during the collision. The horse was put down right there out on the track and carted away in a pick-up. The Magician tried to tell them about the medication and the doctors, but they were too busy stuffing Maxi Pads into his newspaper. Carl and I watched as he mumbled about new prescriptions, better prescriptions, and the feeling of bliss, of God, but he couldn't find anyone like that on the night shift. We found his dead spider plants sprouting fruit flies in his apartment after he didn't show up for three nights straight. Uncle Al said let him go, let the fucker go. He's probably in a McDonald's somewhere asking for change or offering a blowjob. Probably lying in a ditch drinking rainwater again or locked inside a motel room with his pants undone and the television on mute. This time he phoned us from a hardware store.

They call it a youth centre out here in Barrie. They call it a
place for people who have been rundown, people with nowhere
else to go. No one looks sixteen here, not with rotting cheeks,
tired eyes and yellow spots along their legs where the bruises have
begun to heal. The Dillson Motel couldn't keep the Magician
anymore, not after he tried to pawn the shower head and let the
water flood out half the first floor. The Magician is not sixteen, not
even close, but he looks younger than he should. Maybe it's the
patchy nature of that moustache, the way it gathers in tiny bris-
tled bunches on the edges of his cheeks. He is on the floor now
and he's rolling in the French fries, the bone white French fries
he bummed off some kid across the room who keeps asking us
if we are here to take him too. No, no, Carl says, we're just here
for the Magician, we're just here for our cousin and the kid says
they call him Chester the Molester 'cause he looks fucking forty,
doesn't he? Look at him. That ain't no Magician, man, no way.
That's Chester.

Uncle Al kicked the Magician out after he got a hold of some
credit cards and crashed the third Volvo towards the end of high
school. The Magician said it didn't matter, he fucking hated horses
anyway, hated their smell, hated their eyes, hated the way people
talked about them like they were people. They weren't fucking
people; they were commodities like bonds or real estate. They were
property and you were lying to yourself if you said you truly loved
a horse. It'd be like loving your china cabinet or a fifteen percent
increase in your stock portfolio. Like loving a toaster or a Toyota.
Uncle Al loved horses so much, the Magician said, because he could
always decide when to put a bullet between their eyes.

The Magician called every few weeks for cash and always
found new ways to spend it. He got the snake tattoos from some
Estonian girl in Scarborough, along with the hepatitis and whatever else was on the old needles she shared with her sister and their
brother-in-law. The Magician picked up little tattered pieces from
everyone and he clutched them until the stains were his too, until

they all smelled the same. He collected all the spare parts he could find, even if they were busted.

Carl and I pull the Magician up off the floor and he smiles at us. The teeth that are left are bright and white. He might have stolen more white strips from a pharmacy or grocery store. The staff say he has to go; this is a youth shelter, not a hospital ward. Carl waves them off. The Magician yawns and tells me he is tired. He is so tired and he makes his body go limp in our arms. Carl and I buckle under the load and then we are outside in the snow and I can barely see the car. The Magician is still wearing his cargo shorts and that Woodbine T-shirt, but he isn't shivering. His skin is turning pink. He shakes awake in our arms, but doesn't try to move his feet. We drag two parallel lines behind us in the snow. The air smells like McDonald's fries and vinegar. The Magician mumbles in my ear that we should go watch a movie, go hide out in a theatre for a couple of hours. Only a couple hours until he can feel his feet again. His moustache is filling up with white flakes. He wants to know where we are going.

He asks Carl if he remembers watching *Death Wish*, if he remembers Charles Bronson holding that gun to a mugger's head on the subway. He asks about that power, about the will it must take to kill a man. Easy enough to put a horse out of its misery if you have to—if you must. Easy enough to pull that trigger even if you aren't Charles Bronson, even if your hands aren't steady. My hands are getting cold, we're all turning different shades of pink out here, but Carl can't find the keys to the Chevy and the Magician wants to tell us more about horses. He wants to tell us about the best way to feed horses and about Charles Bronson iii, the strongest of all creatures, the noblest of the beasts. He says he will ride again. Carl isn't listening; he's trying to find the keys somewhere in his jacket. The swirling snow bites at my ears and all I can see is the Magician moving his lips, trying to speak. Every word is swallowed by the wind, drowned out by a howl from somewhere down the highway. Somewhere cold. The Magician smells like McDonald's and his eyes are pink around the edges. His lips keep making frosted words.

I can't hear a thing he says.

IN A CAR IN A RIVER
OUTSIDE PEORIA, ILLINOIS

THE FUNDS FROM THE CHURCH WERE DEPOSITED IN HER NAME. THE assets he couldn't hide in Cayman banks or Swiss accounts were placed in safety deposit boxes that only she could open. The countless dollars invested by friends, family and parishioners—all of it floating in offshore bank accounts or squandered on those women out in Reno, the ones who will lick the salty tears off your face for five hundred dollars an hour. The endless shrimp he swallowed as his belly grew wider and wider, the gold watches he lost in cabs and limos with rented drivers and tinted windows. Albert Kale wants to apologize for all of this. He wants to make amends, but at the moment he is still struggling to breathe as water filters through the windows of his '87 Camaro, a gift from his wife on their twentieth anniversary. It was his favourite car in their whole garage.

Albert Kale still believes drowning is less painful than hanging from his belt in a jail cell, swinging like some meaty pendulum. Albert Kale believes they would find him with his feet pointing north in the morning like a compass, a reminder of greater constants, of things beyond our brief reckoning here. He believes drowning will be less painful than a prolonged trial, than all those weeks on the stand, than facing the crowds that once came to worship in the house he built for the Lord. Albert Kale isn't sure if he still believes in God. He knows death in this car in this river won't happen in front of an audience. It won't leave a bright red arc behind.

The water in this car is cold and it is up to Albert's neck now. He keeps his seatbelt on because this is still supposed to be an accident. His heart pills, his liver pills, his pills for a back broken by one of his horses down in Louisville—they float around him in the car like spent confetti. Albert Kale knows he could have swallowed those pills in large handfuls. He has done it before in hotel rooms and on private ranches. Albert Kale is familiar with his pharmaceuticals, but he has no need for them now. He wants his system to be clean when they dredge this river outside his hometown, the river where all the kids used to swim and pitch bottles at passing boats until some girl on water skis took a Heineken in the eye and the cops started patrolling the shore.

Albert Kale remembers his friend Jonah telling him it didn't hurt to drown. He told him it was like drifting off to sleep, like suffocating in a dream, like falling forever. Albert Kale believed Jonah because they were nine years old and Jonah was from Austin and his Mom never went to church. Albert Kale believed him because Jonah claimed he had once fallen off a fishing boat in the Gulf of Mexico, back when his Dad still lived with his Mom and they had two televisions in the house. As he drifted below the water, Jonah claimed, the fish followed him down from the surface. Their silvery shapes began to spell out his name as his chest filled with water. Jonah said it didn't hurt, not until after. It was one of the Mexican labourers on the boat who pulled him out, who pushed the water out of his lungs and brought him back to life. Afterward, Jonah's father told him all the splashing scared away anything worth catching.

Jonah called sometimes from halfway houses on the Louisiana coast. He called asking to speak to his old friend Albert Kale. He called because Albert's ads were all over TV down there, pictures of his benevolent face radiating calm, collected understanding. Albert Kale understood. He understood why a man might hit his wife, why he might cheat on his taxes, steal from his neighbour, or even bury his own child in the backyard without a marker to signify the crime. Albert Kale understood the weak and weeping masses that poured into his holy church on the second and fourth Sundays after the welfare cheques came out. He understood them all.

The water begins to burble around Albert's mouth and he considers undoing the seatbelt, but his hands are too cold. Jonah said they were still running the church's ads alongside reports about Albert's crimes, about the money that disappeared and all those people he promised salvation for a dollar ninety-five a day. Jonah called because all those sermons seemed to drip with the same words he told Albert—back when they were kids, back when Jonah couldn't spell methamphetamine and didn't like the taste of cold medicine. Albert hung up on him, but Jonah did not stop calling. He wanted Albert Kale to know about the two years in juvenile detention, about solitude and ping-pong and what it meant to be alone, surrounded by men with old teeth, new wounds and no fixed address.

Albert Kale wants to keep breathing, but the water continues to slip through the cracks of his Camaro. He wants to rethink his options, reapply whatever twisted logic forced him to plunge his vehicle into the water this cold November. He wants to emerge from this enlightened, but the pressure keeps the doors shut. The locks have shorted out and his arms are so tired. His wife will not forgive him for this. She will smile because that is what she does, but she won't forgive him.

Albert Kale has no ID in his wallet. He can't reach his back pocket to check, but he knows it isn't there. It's on a nightstand somewhere with all his old receipts. Albert Kale wants someone to remember what his face looks like before it bloats beneath the water, before all the fluids in his body begin to turn to gas. His face won't look like it does on the billboards scattered throughout the Midwest, the ones staggered up and down the back roads and the highways through dead and depleted towns. His face in these ads is clean-shaven. His chins are tucked beneath a bright white collar. It's his eyes though that cause motorists to pause, that cause men and women in motels without bibles to dial the 1-800 number. They imagine those eyes staring at them like a beacon as they clutch the phone against their neck and listen to Prince after the dial tone, waiting for Albert Kale's voice to tell them about the fish spelling out his name beneath the water, the ones who told him it didn't hurt to drown or die.

It was like falling through a dream, he would tell them. Like being lifted up again.

Albert Kale knows Jonah has called this number. Even as the water covers his eyes and small air pockets begin to escape from his nose, he can only think about Jonah calling that number to hear Albert Kale tell his story about the fish and the drowning sensation. Except in Albert's version, it's his father who saves him. There is no Mexican labourer—no one thought that would sit well with the listeners. Jonah would call and find Albert Kale there, telling his story in that calm and collected voice, the same one Albert used in interviews with journalists and state's attorneys and the old lady from 20/20.

Jonah would call asking for Albert, asking if it really was his father. Jonah remembered Albert's father as a hard man, a man who kicked them out of the attic, who stole cigarettes from his neighbours' cars and once rabbit punched a teenager in line at the liquor store. The police said it cracked two vertebrae, but no one ever identified the attacker. Jonah wanted to know who this father was and why there was no Mexican labourer on that boat. Jonah called and called until he spoke to Albert Kale himself. Jonah said he wanted to talk. He wanted to know why.

It does not feel like a dream. Albert Kale's arms and legs begin to spasm and shake in the water as his body fights for air, for a surface he can't reach. The roof of the car will not budge against his balding head. It is not like drifting off to sleep. There is no one here to grab him. Albert Kale is collapsing from the inside out. Maybe a passing driver will spot his bright red car floating in the river. Maybe no one will notice the bits of Jonah's shirt still clinging to the undercarriage. Albert Kale knows there will be no one there to judge him after this car finally sinks. Jonah asked him for credit, as if his story about those fish in the Gulf wasn't a lie, some old concoction from a child's mind. Jonah just wanted all the things Albert Kale had, all the things now slipping through his fingers, all those things trapped inside this car.

Albert just wants this to look like an accident. He wants to tell Jonah—what's left of Jonah on the bloody floor of that parking garage—this was all an accident. Each cell in Albert's body screams for air as his lungs swallow up the brackish water. There are no fish left in this river. They all died back when Albert's father worked at the mill, back before all of this began to crumble, before Jonah said this was a peaceful way to die. He always was a liar.

CLOUD

EVERYTHING IS COVERED IN SHIT.

When the birds first arrived, everyone was taking pictures. Jimmy and I rode our bikes down the streets, pointing at houses covered in starlings. They looked like oil slicks spreading from roof to roof. The trees were filled with their chirping babies and the sky would occasionally go dark when they rose together in flight. News teams and professional photographers clogged up the downtown taking photos of the phenomenon. They split it straight across their tongues and spat it at the camera. They were all so proud of our new bird collection.

Phenomenon—they said it like we were special.

Everyone is gone now of course. Hudson is just the bird town now. We are a freak show—we would be listed in some tourist's top ten destinations if it wasn't for all the poop. Our cars are covered in white bird shit; it eats straight through the paint. Half the kids in town have something wrong with their lungs. We are choking on air filled with feathers and feces. Most of my brother's friends carry around inhalers and wear surgical masks when they go outside. I tie a bandana around my face and wear a hat to keep their constant droppings out of my hair. Jimmy wears his Dad's motorcycle helmet and has to keep Windexing the visor.

We are told by parks officials and some short fat man from the government this all will pass, but the birds don't seem to agree. They gather in large patches in our front yards and observe us through the glass. They rattle our windows in the morning and sing songs to one another when we try to sleep. They almost never blink and all their eyes look like spilled change. They steal tinfoil and barrettes and old batteries from our garages. They eat our garbage and they do not look away. Sometimes they rise and fall like a tide through the air, blocking out the sun and swallowing the rain. You can hear their wings beat in unison. They have no rhythm though—just a buzzing noise like grinding teeth. No matter where you go, the birds are always watching.

"What you two want gas for?" Orlando says. He carries an umbrella over his head outside the gas station booth. It is already spotted with droppings. Orlando runs the station and owns two others down by the highway. He sometimes details Jimmy's Mom's car to keep the shit from ruining her paint job. The three of us stand around the pump and try to fill the gas can. Jimmy and I found it after school in a janitor's closet. The cleaning staff kind of gave up when the birds arrived and a lot of people decided to pull out of town. No one will notice that it's gone.

"We need it for the lawn mower. You know, to cut the grass," Jimmy says.

"What grass? Birds been shitting all of it to death. Too much fertilizer."

Orlando isn't wrong. Most of the grass in town is already dead. Trees and plants are losing their leaves. My parents spend their weekends trapping the starlings in cages paid for by the government. They kill the birds by applying thoracic compression, according to my Dad. Basically, you squeeze them to death with your hands. You wear gloves and you wait until their hearts explode or their lungs collapse or whatever comes first, I guess. My parents are paid by the pound and are told to put the birds in plastic garbage bags. Every Monday two garbage trucks roll down the streets and collect whatever people could catch that week. All the bags are splattered with bird shit by the morning. The birds have begun to figure out the traps.

"Well, we can still ride on the mower, can't we?" Jimmy says and hands Orlando five bucks. Orlando shakes his head and starts to dart back toward his booth. The glass walls are covered with pictures of Jimmy Buffett and ocean views. Jimmy says Orlando only wishes he was from Florida. He is too pale. He would burn up if the birds ever left and the sun came back again. Sometimes we catch him trying to play guitar at night. He sings from inside the booth at the top of his lungs. You can't hear anything over the birds though, so he just looks like a mime.

We strap the gas can into the basket on the front of Jimmy's bike. His Mom doesn't know about our plan, but we stash a lot of our stuff at her place. My parents have taken over our garage with nets and cages and the stench of rotting feathers. Orlando tries to yell something after us about safety, but we are already gone, our legs pumping the pedals down the speckled streets. Small children watch us from the windows and above us the thrum of wings remains unending. We live permanently under a cloud and breathe filtered air. We are the only people outside and we would not have it any other way. We will not be cowed by all these fucking birds.

"This is not going to work. We need a longer hose or something. Maybe a bigger motor or like a water gun kind of thing. Air pressure? You're supposed to be good at science, Tony."

The birds only killed one man since they arrived. I mean, they're slowly killing us all, I'm sure, but this was almost premeditated according to Jimmy. This was a homicide.

"Look, I can go back to your place and take a look if you want, but I don't know if a hose is going to do it. We might be better just trying an oxygen tank or something."

"And where are going to get one of those?" Jimmy says.

We are in the woods behind Jimmy's place. There are birds in the trees around us, but they keep scattering whenever we start up the mower. It was Jimmy's idea to build this machine. Something like a flamethrower on wheels to clear out the sky. Something to burn up all these winged oil spots and put an end to the surgical masks and rain coats. I thought high school was going to be full of girls in skirts and spaghetti straps, but the birds kind of ruined all of that. Everyone is all bundled up. We don't even trust the ceilings inside the school. You can hear the babies squealing for food up in the rafters and down in the empty drains. They invade every space and stuff holes full with wrapping paper and old plastic grocery bags.

"Try and start it up again. I will go back to the house and try to find some more hose."

The trees around me are made of dead branches and slimy bark. Jimmy's backyard is fenced off from the woods, but that doesn't mean the birds don't like to settle in his yard. They hop away from me as I try and skirt around the abandoned barbecue. This was where Jimmy's dad trapped a bunch of them after the last of the news teams began to trickle out of town. Once the cameras realized the birds were here to stay, most of them lost interest. They could always check in with us again in a couple weeks and file a report about the air pollution. The birds would not dictate their schedule. They were free to leave. Jimmy says we should go too, but he's not ready yet. There are still too many birds here in Hudson. There are too many beaks to feed.

It was Jimmy's Dad who was trying to cook steaks out in the backyard with an umbrella over his head when the birds swooped down to poke at his meat. Maybe he didn't realize they were in there when he slammed the lid shut, or maybe he just didn't give a shit. There was a scream at first, apparently. The sky went dark for a second. Jimmy described a cloud of wings and bright eyes descending from the roof to swallow up his father's body in some feathered suit, their tiny beaks piercing his skin. Their shrill squawks drowned out his voice and the air smelled like burning hair, but it was all those feathers in the barbecue. Jimmy's Mom pulled him away from the window. It lasted maybe fifteen minutes until his Dad stopped moving. His Mom was the one who remained composed when the cops arrived to take a statement. She was the one who led them to the corpse. The birds left most of the body behind, but the eyes were gone. The medics carted the body away under a blue tarp, but Jimmy said it still left a wet trail behind. The birds still don't go near the barbecue and Jimmy says all they fear is fire.

I push my way into the garage and look for a longer piece of hose. I don't really think this plan is going to work. If anything, one of us is just going to end up on fire. There really isn't anyone else to hang out with though. Jimmy and I are the only ones who will go outside. Most of the girls stay indoors and phone each other. Sometimes they just sleep or write messages in soap on their windows until the bird shit covers them again. We used to leave all the girls letters about our plan to burn out the sky, but they didn't write back. No one really thinks we can pull it off. I don't really blame them, but Jimmy seems to think girls aren't worth our time anyway.

The garage is full of all his Dad's stuff. Clothes and diplomas and fishing equipment are stacked up against the walls. Jimmy's Mom dumped it all out here after they buried his father just outside town. She lets me stay over most nights when I get tired of listening to my parents strangling as many birds as they can for the government. My little brother says it's like listening to someone treading water forever, but he's a big fan of understatements. He uses headphones to block out the sound, but I swear all the chirping cuts right through the foam. It sounds like popped balloons or piñatas imploding inside the walls around me. It never seems to stop.

I step into the house still searching for the hose. Jimmy's Mom keeps everything clean. There are no dishes in the sink. I sleep on a fold out couch that is tucked away every morning. Everything is in its right place. I move through the house looking for something to

help us spew burning gas into the air. A funnel or a piece of pipe—
there really isn't much to find. Voices clatter down the stairs and I
try to ignore them. With all the birds outside, most of us have to
use the phone to reach each other. Some of the older houses out
here still use a party line. Jimmy's Mom is always on the phone
with someone. I can hear her laughing up there. Then somebody
who sounds like Orlando starts talking about moving and I stop
at the bottom of the stairs.

"Look, I don't need to stay here. I've got money from when my
old man keeled over. He has an old house down in North Carolina
or something. We can move down there, take the kid. I don't really
care what happens. I just can't stay here any longer, Kelly."

"Jimmy won't want to go. He still wants to…"

"What, finish off the birds? No, Kelly, this is a fucking ghost
town. No one is coming back here. Oh, they might come for the
bird anniversary or to take pictures of all the dead shit out here,
but no one is moving into Hudson. We're slowly draining out all
the people until it's just old timers and the poor fuckers who think
they can win against these goddamn starlings. The things repro-
duce faster than you can blink. It's a lost cause."

"I know, I know, alright Orlando? I hear you. You wanna be the
one who tells Jimmy? His Dad's still buried here. All his friends are
here. His school is here. He is still trying to be a kid. He doesn't
even know about you yet and now you wanna move him a thousand miles away?"

I try to sneak out the back door. Their voices are rising, but I
know Orlando's right.

"If it means getting away from this endless rain of shit? Hell
yeah, Kelly."

There is no way we can win. We can only try and run.

"What is it?" Jimmy says. He's got the mower stuck in the mud
again. He's pushing it out of a hole and back up into the clearing.
I try not to say anything, but he grabs me by the shoulder.

"You couldn't find the hose or what? Come on, Tony. Do I have to do everything? Jesus."

Jimmy starts stomping off towards the house, but I call after him.

"You don't wanna go back there, man. Let's just finish up here and then..."

"What's your problem, man?" Jimmy turns back towards me. He's covered in sweat.

I say nothing and climb onto the mower. I try to back it up into the clearing, but Jimmy grabs the steering wheel. He tries to turn it off, but can't get a handle on the key.

"Look, if you don't wanna do this, that's fine, alright? Just stop making excuses, Tony."

I stop the mower. Jimmy won't stop staring at me. His hands still clench the wheel.

"What is your problem, huh?"

I swallow and try to stare up into the trees.

"Orlando and your Mom—they were talking. They wanna go..."

"Go out, go what? Whatever he wants to do... Look, what is your problem?"

"They wanna move you down to Carolina or something. They wanna get out of town before everyone else leaves and Hudson just dies. And he's right, man. I mean, he has a point."

Jimmy lets go of the wheel and sits down on the ground. I don't move from my seat.

"He thinks he's my Dad? Is that it? I knew he was like, friends with my Mom, or whatever, but... he thinks he can take me down there? When we are doing all this shit here? Did they say anything about my Dad? What did my Mom say? Did she say it was a good idea? She knows that we own this house right? And that you and I are trying to get rid of all these things?"

I don't want to say anything. I try to make eye contact with the birds around us. They are gathered on the branches, but they aren't saying much. I want to crush them in my hands.

"He said he has a house... and I mean, well your Mom wasn't happy, but Orlando kind of had a point. Like, who else goes outside besides us? No one is out there on the street at all."

"That stupid pale fucker," Jimmy says. His face goes red and I can see foam rising in his mouth. He spits onto the ground and I remember when Rachel Henderson shot him down in the fourth grade. He took all her pencil crayons and ran each one through the sharpener at recess until only shavings remained. Jimmy pulls his Dad's motorcycle helmet and slams the visor shut.

"Nobody wants to fucking help. They're all too busy planning with each other."

Jimmy takes off into the woods and I'm left sitting on the lawn mower. The birds begin to cackle around me. I fire up the mower and try to ride it out of the woods. I want to follow him and explain this was all a mistake. We can still finish this project. We can still burn out the sky.

The mower gets stuck in the mud again and I am forced to walk.

Eventually, I catch up to Jimmy at Orlando's gas station. He has smashed all the glass and is tearing down the pictures when I arrive. White sand beaches and Jimmy Buffett's moustache flutter away into the wind past my face. The birds circle above the destruction, but refuse to swoop down for a closer look. Jimmy tears apart every image as I approach. He is still wearing his helmet and it is splotched with white arcs of shit. He turns and spots me riding toward him with the gas can dangling from my handlebars. He raises two middle fingers in my direction and runs toward his bike. I drop the gas can and keep pedalling. My lungs are filled with phlegm.

"We aren't finished yet!" I scream through my bandanna. "We aren't done! Come back! You can stay with me, man! You can stay, alright?"

Jimmy keeps pedalling away from me. His legs have always been stronger than mine. He thinks he can outrun this cloud. I scream after him as my muscles begin to surrender. They burn and burn and eventually I have to stop before I throw up or pass out into a ditch. Jimmy tosses up a tail of dust behind him as he hits the road out of town. He passes the sign welcoming everyone to Hudson. He passes the graveyard where they put his father and all our grandparents. He thinks he can beat them, that he can escape the cloud lingering above us all. Jimmy passes the final corner toward the highway. I can only see the glint of his black helmet now. He thinks he's gone.

I look up into the sky above me. Everything is black and the wings go on forever.

GOD IS A PLACE

CALEB TAKES THE BABY WHILE TWINK IS AT WORK. HE BUNDLES IT up in sweaters and wraps it in a bath towel. He doesn't trust the baby, and he doesn't believe it's his child. It burps and squeals while he tries to sleep in the other room. It drains the life out of Twink from her tits, sapping all that warm rich life away into piss and shit and other fluids. Twink's night shifts stretch out into the early hours before dawn, where the old men ask her if she's queer and ponder aloud why she was named after a pastry in the first place. Twink is nowhere to be found in those early hours and so Caleb is the one sitting at home, listening to the squealing mass, the baby she says is his, but it does not have his eyes, it does not have his long, bony hands and it never shuts up. It squeals for milk that is too warm, too cold, too much. There is always too much.

Caleb can't get the prescription he needs and his left knee is still broken somewhere deep inside, somewhere deep and unknowable, according to the doctors who hold out soft, soft hands for their coins and cheques and endless pounds of flesh. The darkness is the same way and so Caleb continues down his path with the baby clutched in his arms, dodging streetlights and the occasional cab that slows to pass him on the shoulder. Everyone will have their piece eventually. Everyone will take a piece of the whole, punishing the body for the sins of the hand.

Caleb's hands are red in the cold and he worries they will draw out wandering eyes. They are glowing and he can barely feel them. The baby is quiet; maybe it is freezing too. The cold is not an enemy. It is a warm embrace that articulates each breath you take. Caleb stops to lean against a tree to whisper something about St. Peter choking on a stone. All your idols are crumbling, he warns the baby and the baby cries because it knows Caleb is right and so Caleb says, you weren't born from me. And the baby cries again.

Caleb fell off the top shelf of the pasta aisle at the grocery store a year ago. Twink was working the cash and she took him to the hospital and filed the workman's comp and got them both kicked out of her Mom's place once the baby bump could not be hidden anymore. She said it was Caleb's, but Caleb can't remember getting hard, not after his knee blew out and so he says okay, but it really isn't okay. He remembers another boy and another bottle and not drinking. He doesn't want the new apartment with the ducts and pipes filtering fluids and air through their bedroom, the stove rattling every time the bus stops in front of the house. He doesn't want the feet shuffling above him or the loud screams of raccoons mating in the attic. Fighting, mating, all the same things; all flesh on flesh and the baby is just flesh, that's it.

Caleb remembers a church group and being able to walk without a limp and his older brother telling them about Jesus carrying you when you were suffering, when life was hard and filled with stones that cut the bottoms of your feet. Caleb has forgotten to wear his shoes and his socks are soaked and growing stiff around his toes. His brother was a youth pastor and a saviour and always right until the police took everyone away because of the incident, and so Caleb focuses on the baby instead, the one in his arms, the one that isn't his and he tells the baby it will be okay even though he's in the park now and the snow is deeper than he thought. He tells the baby to breathe with him and that Twink will be better after this, she will be less sad, she will be so much better. She will find them locked in time, locked in place, held together by moisture in the air because that's where God is. God is a place. God is a place you will wait for the rest of your life.

Two joggers will find them in the morning cold and the baby still won't have a name.

SELF-CLEANING OVEN

AFTER THE THIRD ATTEMPT, HARRIET'S SISTERS STARTED TO CALL her the self-cleaning oven. Henry already had one kid with Doris, the bitch who kept calling them in the middle of the night to complain about the water temperature in Henry's old house. She still expected him to maintain the property even after receiving full custody of their mewling little Jamie. Henry began sleeping through the phone calls and so it was Harriet who had to answer the phone.

"Stop. Just stop, Doris. Call a plumber. Just look it up online."

Three years with Henry and the calls still continued. Three years and three miscarriages.

Harriet's sisters asked her if she had read the books they gave her. The one's about sleeping on your back for all nine months and eating only cucumbers or avocados. They asked if she was smoking cigarettes when no one else was looking. They checked her cabinets for secret stashes of whiskey and questioned Henry. Was he beating her? Did he have a history of malformed sperm? Harriet just wanted them to go away, but they had nothing else to distract them.

Theresa had her tubes tied after the third kid came out in one swift motion in a bus station bathroom and Deidra already had two kids in college. She never bothered finding another man after Bob was hit with two heart attacks in a row while cutting the lawn. It was Harriet, the youngest, who was lagging behind. Their mother would not have been impressed. Harriet's sisters visited the grave-yard once a week to talk to their mother's marble gravestone and Harriet was pretty sure all they did was discuss how the youngest Donoghue had failed the family. They even brought letters about her to read. Harriet discovered them when she showed up with flowers on her mother's birthday. Pieces of paper fluttering around the cemetery, listing all her faults and failures chronologically with footnotes and everything. It was a long list.

The phone rings again and Harriet picks it up. Doris is on the other end again.

"Do you think I have the money for a plumber? Do you real-ize how expensive this dump is to heat once October hits? It ain't cheap, I can tell you that much. And if you hang up on me again, I swear to God—"

Harriet leaves the phone off the hook and rolls over to go back to sleep. Henry does not move. He has become impervious to noise. Harriet closes her eyes and tries to dream of a plant that will never die. All she can find are cactuses that stretch up into the clouds.

In the morning, she drives by the old house Henry surrendered to Doris during the divorce. The windows are covered in dust and half the trim has begun to rot away. Henry is still only allowed to see the boy on weekend visits with a social worker present. A minor sex offender conviction when he was in high school has become a ghost, a fifteen-year-old girl floating over every conversation; her parents demanded an officer press the charges.

This ghost appears at random, unravelling the many lives Henry's tried to build since they were caught in her basement without pants or excuses. It pokes holes in resumes and drives away investors from his growing hot tub empire. It sulks in corners and lashes out in courtrooms and custody battles. Henry tells Harriet she would like his son, but he's not allowed to bring anyone to the visits. Doris has filed a petition about corrupting influences. She isn't wrong exactly. Harriet is the one who broke up their marriage, the one who slowly pulled Henry away from a life of baseball games and barbecues and cold bed sheets. Harriet is the one who diagnosed their marriage, the one who reached inside and pulled out a heart crusted in bile. She does not regret any of it, but sometimes she does regret there was a child. Doris holds him up like a trophy and the doctor says Henry's sperm are still energetic, still thriving. Harriet wants to blame it all on the hot tubs, but the doctor says that isn't the case. She tries to avoid thinking about other options. She focuses on Doris and what she would look like floating face down in a hot tub.

The boy is sitting on the porch with a deflated basketball. He tries to bounce it off the concrete steps, but it barely reacts. Harriet pulls over and watches him try to blow air into the tiny hole. The kid's face turns red and then purple before he surrenders and tosses the ball away into the overgrown grass. Harriet rolls down the window and yells out into the street.

"You're Henry's kid, right?"

The boy is only six. He doesn't say anything at first. He stands on the steps and looks toward the front door, but doesn't move. Harriet climbs out of the car. She remembers all those public service announcements about strangers in cars. No matter what her sisters say, Harriet knows she is not a monster. She just doesn't always think things through. Henry says it wasn't her fault that they fired her from the cereal factory, but he doesn't know about the lift she dropped on Debbie Anderson or the medical bills her family has to pay. Harriet doesn't think he'd want to know. She bought a hot tub from him with some of the severance money. After all, nobody could prove Harriet was definitely the one who dropped that lift on Debbie. Debbie didn't have a lot of friends on the inside of that place. She liked to take naps in the bathroom and smoke in the loading bay, leaving her butts behind for security to find on the midnight shift. She had it coming, Harriet told her sisters. They asked if it was an accident. Of course it was, Harriet said.

"Don't worry, don't worry, I'm just your Dad's friend," Harriet says. The kid looks for his basketball in the grass. He won't look her in the eye as she steps toward him.

"You're Jamie, right? Don't worry; your Dad and I are close. Where is your Mom?"

The boy nods, but doesn't say anything.

"Is she at work? Is she still working at the mall?"

"Yeah," Jamie says. He's still looking for his ball in the grass.

"And she just leaves you here all day?"

He nods again. The driveway is cracked and filled with weeds. Crabgrass and dandelions border its edges. Harriet wants to pluck them up, but she resists. Doris might notice. She seems to keep a record of everything. She probably has a photo of every single plant out here.

"Well, isn't there like a babysitter or someone?"

Jamie stares up at her. He looks like a chubbier Henry.

"Sometimes. At night, yeah. But the sun is out."

Harriet knows she should call Henry. Some proof of neglect, a way to get the courts to take his side against Doris. All Doris has to do is summon up his high school ghost, but now they have something substantial on their side. There is no guardian in sight. No one to watch the kid.

"The sun is out, yeah. Your Mom says that's alright?"

Jamie nods again and tries to bounce the ball. It doesn't even bother hopping away this time.

"How about you come with me for the day? We can do whatever we want. How does that sound to you? You want to go somewhere for lunch or something?"

Doris gets the kid and the house. Doris seems to get everything but Henry. And all Henry seems to do these days is sleep. He is slowly falling apart in front of her, no matter what the doctor says. Maybe her sisters are right. Maybe there is something wrong with him, something she just can't see yet. Harriet grabs Jamie by the hand and they walk toward her car. She is tired of trying for a kid like Jamie. She just wants someone to hand her one already, fully formed.

"Okay, but we have to come back soon or she will be mad."

Harriet knows she can handle the pain.

The restaurant is one of those off-brand waffle house places that sprout up like fungus along highway exit ramps. Jamie has five Belgian waffles in front him, piled with bananas, strawberries and whipped cream. Harriet only has a coffee. Her sisters say the caffeine is going to destroy her heart eventually. The restaurant is close to empty and everything is sticky.

"I don't think I can eat all of this, Harriet."

"You can do your best, that's all anyone can ask for, Jamie."

Harriet feels bad lying to the kid. Her best is rarely ever acceptable. Henry seems to tolerate her attempts at least. He was there at the hospital every time her body had turned against her, poisoning itself against the future she was trying to create. He brought her food from outside the hospital, sneaking in chocolates and real egg salad sandwiches. The hospital used powder eggs. Harriet refused to swallow any institution's food. She didn't trust the nurses. They all looked too much like her mother, all knowing eyes and cooing voices hiding their contempt.

"Are you going to eat any of these?"

"I think you can handle it," Harriet says. The kid is well behaved. He didn't even try to change the radio station on the way over. They talk about basketball and stepping on Lego in the dark. Jamie asks her what she did for a job and Harriet says it's none of his business. He doesn't seem to mind. His Mom cuts hair at the mall and brings home a lot of coins inside her purse. Harriet smiles. Maybe it could be this easy. If only she could get her body to agree for once, to lend her a pass. Jamie tries to pour syrup on his waffles and misses the plate entirely. Harriet sops it up in one motion and throws the napkin on the floor. Let the waiter clean it up.

"I think I need to sleep, Harriet."

"We will take you home in a bit, okay? I'm sure your Mom will be looking for you."

Doris won't be able to explain this. She just needs to draw it out a bit longer. And Harriet likes Jamie. He might not be a clean eater, but he hasn't crapped himself or done anything stupid yet. All the awful years have already passed, including the terrible twos. When he gets into his teens there will be problems, but Henry can handle that. Henry is good with those kinds of situations. He is the one who handles Harriet's sisters when they come by to ask about her stomach, her health, her future plans. Henry is very good at slamming doors.

"When my Dad comes over, he and my Mom talk about you sometimes."

Harriet stops drinking her coffee. She pours more sugar into the grainy remains.

"What do you mean, Jamie? Is your Mom still mad at me? You know, you can't always trust everything a grown-up says. You have to learn what to believe. It's hard to know sometimes."

"I know," Jamie says. His eyes are drooping and he misses his mouth with a fork of waffle.

"Well, what do they say Jamie? Is your Mom upset about something?"

Jamie stabs at his food again, but can't bother to raise the fork.

"They say they just want you to go away. I wanna lie down. Can I lie down?"

Harriet doesn't answer. She places both hands on the sticky table and closes her eyes. Henry said the visits with Doris always devolved into some screaming match about the drapes or the water heater. Harriet never asked why they took so long. She never asked about the social worker or the supervised visitations. There were messages Henry deleted from the answering machine before Harriet could listen. There were long car drives and strange clothes in the trunk. Harriet always wrote it off as part of the business—selling hot tubs wasn't like selling pens or hair clippers. Harriet pulls her sticky hands off the table. Jamie has curled up in the booth with whipped cream in his hair. She wants to reach over and wipe it away, but her hand won't let her.

With every attempt she and Henry made for a child, Harriet had tried to erase the malformed image of the last one—the twisted hands and half-formed faces. She pushed Debbie Anderson's crushed legs from her mind, the screams echoing up the delivery shaft at the factory. She clenched Henry's body between her legs and drowned out her prying sisters with moans to rattle the bedroom. Henry's grunts helped hide the fear humming inside her diaphragm, rattling her organs. She could almost negate her mother's voice from beyond the grave, the one tapping at the window, begging to ask about her grandchildren, her legacy. She had left so much behind. Harriet had filled her mind with one desire, for a wriggling thing made of flesh and blood to take up a space inside her, to call it her own. She just wanted something new, something no one had used yet. Henry didn't fit the bill—he never really had. Doris wasn't finished with him yet.

Jamie is still asleep when Harriet stands up from the table. The waiter is flirting with some hostess near the back. There are no other customers. She takes a few steps away from the sticky table. Jamie does not move; he only snores. She clenches her hands around her purse and walks toward the door. Harriet does not want Doris' child. She does not want Henry's leftovers. She wants to ask Henry if she was just a distraction, to ask him why he's always drawn back to the same fire, the one Doris keeps lighting between them.

Harriet steps outside into the parking lot. No one has followed her outside. The sun is out and, somewhere, Doris is still at work, cutting hair, talking shit, talking about Harriet and her poisoned womb. Too much time in those hot tubs, she will say. Too much time in that putrid, tacky hot tub Henry purchased as their honeymoon gift. It was bright pink, you know—such an ugly looking thing. Harriet climbs into her car and slams the door. Jamie sleeps alone inside the restaurant, surrounded by waffles with eyes and mouths mounted on the walls.

Harriet starts the car and pulls onto the highway. She tosses soiled tissues out the window and tries not to look back. She waits for the police to pull her over as the miles turn into hours.

Harriet is driving until she finds a desert. Any one will do.

A BIRD IN THE HAND
IS WORTHLESS

THREE HOURS AFTER WE BOOST THE TV, CAL STARTS TALKING ABOUT going to California. He talks about the girls with those tits you find online, the ones who never have to bundle up for the winter 'cause the sun never sets on Burbank or Malibu or any of those places. He talks about bottomless margaritas and endless shrimp buffets, room service and escorts you can pay by the minute. Cal says he will teach me to surf, teach me everything.

I'm trying to figure out where we'll unload this Panasonic for more than a hundred bucks, so I try to ignore him. I don't even think Cal remembered to grab the remote before we left the Stockyard. He's only been bouncing there for two weeks and Big Randy doesn't tell him shit. Just says to keep sticky fingers off the girls and watch for those assholes with the spy cameras tucked up under their hats. They're the ones ruining the profits.

"The best part is no snow. No ice. No waking up at night with your balls shrunk to prunes."

No way am I getting the kids back if someone finds us with this TV. No one's going to report a missing TV these days. Not when we left how many thousands tucked inside Randy's office, covered in white powder and protein stains or whatever else is dripping from the DJ's nose. The report will just go into a file folder somewhere in the station basement until the annual Christmas bonfire consumes it all.

"You ever think about learning to surf, Jimmy? I seen too many guys bust their faces on America's Funniest Home Videos to try that shit, but maybe if I hired a trainer…"

The lawyer says motions take money to file, and I got a lot of motions to make. I've got pictures I went and printed off at the library. Pictures of Alice doing shots of tequila in Georgia, pictures of long salt lines stretching up her stomach and down the sides of her hips. She's lost weight and her nose is red. Every time she smiles, the camera burns her eyes a little deeper until they're just holes. She's got denim jeans on down there in Florida, sleeping every night in Brad Paisley's tour bus. No snow to keep her shrivelled and cold. She says she's in love, says he's the one, ever since they met at the Havelock Jamboree. Lawyer says I need to file each piece of evidence separately, but his office smells like cat piss and the law degree hanging from his wall is missing some punctuation. He drives a Buick with three bald tires and smiles too much when I step into his office. Alice keeps posting pictures from down in the Keys, her arms wrapped around bodyguards, her tattoos of Jason and Marlee poking out from under the straps of her bathing suit while she sips champagne and the sun sets like it's the end of the world behind her.

I am waiting for her camera to break.

"Cal, let's take it to Donna."

Cal looks up from his fantasies of ten-pound shrimp and naked eighteen-year-olds. He needs his pills to stay lucid and awake, but he doesn't get paid until we sell this piece of shit. I can't carry a TV by myself.

"Whatever you wanna do, man. She might still be up."

The road is pockmarked and swallows up my front tire as we bounce away from the arena parking lot. The streetlights guide me and I try to spin the radio dial away from country stations where Paisley sings about mud on the tires, Southern girls and the endless bounty of America. All I can see is Alice writhing on the stage under some kind of smoke machine and a bunch of cigarettes burning in the audience before her, burning until I start to cough. A stoplight pulses into my vision and reminds me to make a left onto the busted gravel. Only one set of lights glows down the row of bungalows. There are snowmen watching us as we pass.

Donna used to work with Alice at the Stockyard back before Paisley and his tour bus. Her old boy Delany got her some Oxys after he was run off the road a few months ago by the cops. They keep her from dreaming, she says. Keep her from all the boys leering in her sleep. She's always got cash laying around, tucked between underwear and couch cushions. No bank account. I have Cal knock at the door and try not to let her see me standing beside him in the cold.

The Panasonic sits in the backseat and stares at us.

"Five in the morning, Cal. Five in the goddamn morning. You got some need? I don't have anything for it. Told you that once before. Now get off my porch before I wake up Del."

"We got something for you, Donna. Why you always gotta spin it back at me?"

Donna leans her head out the door into the cold. Her hair is wet.

"Oh hell no. Fuck that. You wanna bring that asshole in here?"

I jam a hand into the doorframe before Donna can close it.

"We'll make it worth your while, alright? I promise I won't do any crazy shit."

Donna knows all about the phone calls. She knows about the messages I left on Alice's voicemail, the ones that allowed her parents to come and grab the kids. Alice played them for her. I told the officers I wasn't in a very good state of mind at the time. Alice played them for everybody, even got me suspended from the mill for a month. That didn't stop the bills though, and it didn't stop the lawyer. Voice mail ruined all of that. Voice mail and Brad Paisley's hairless chest.

"Yeah? You won't—what was it—string me up like a kite? Chop me up so I'll fit down the drain better? What else did you say to her? You'd lock the kids up in a hole before you'd let her touch them? Got enough holes on your property to do that, Jimmy. Got enough holes to bury everyone if you wanted to. Get off my porch."

Cal turns back to the car.

"Hey, grab that thing and show her off. Don't just run," I say.

Headlights roll up the street, and Cal skitters back up to the porch.

"I can't get fired again, man. If they find out about this—"

"About what?' Donna says. Her hair is starting to freeze and my hand turns red inside the doorframe. "You really got something for me, or is this all just bullshit to figure out where Alice is at now?"

"We actually have something," I say and the pressure loosens up off my fist. I crack my knuckles and look at the damage. Donna shakes the ice in her hair and we follow the droplets down the hall. Her living room is stacked with magazines and lingerie and all the furniture is orange. Donna lives inside a pumpkin, and her TV is a piece of shit.

"Two hundred bucks for a Panasonic. Thirty-two inches of glory. What do you say?"

Donna flips through a magazine and ignores us on the couch. Cal is pacing back and forth. He needs to get back to his apartment before he starts freaking out again. Twenty years dealing with Cal and I never understood why he won't carry his meds on him.

"Not even a scratch on it, alright? You can replace this piece of crap and save yourself five hundred bucks in the process. Cash. Right now. All we gotta do is pull it outta the backseat."

Sometimes Donna babysat Jason and Marlee. She used to play hide and seek with them until Marlee climbed into the dryer and hid there for a few hours. Alice almost took off Donna's head when she came home from a shift covered in cold sweat and make-up to find her daughter banging on the lint trap. After that, it was just movies and board games.

"Can you keep your voice down, Jimmy? You're gonna wake up Del. He's supposed to find out tomorrow if they'll let him do any physio after the trial is done. Doesn't want to be a cripple forever—Cal get your hands off of that shit. I'm air drying those things."

Cal takes a seat and pulls out some postcards he jacked from the gas station. He's written letters to his mother across the back with fake addresses stretching up and down the Golden Coast. It's the only excuse he can think of to avoid the hospital. Cal can't handle hospitals—too many reflective surfaces, too many people asking how he feels today, asking for reasons and for his personal information. His Mom is only twenty minutes down the highway, but it may as well be Florida for all he cares.

"Who gives a shit about Del?" I say. "He shouldn't have run. They catch him with three or four plants in the car, so what? Could plead that down. Get off with some probation."

Donna rolls her eyes at me. While I was plotting murders in Alice's inbox to try and win her back, Del had been trying to move his stash from an abandoned cottage to the family farm. New owners and buyers in the area had everyone a little on edge. Lots of old things lying underneath rotten decks and docks that no one with any sense wanted to find. Del was just trying to do some clean up when the sirens came on behind him. He let them chase him for twenty minutes until they forced him into the ditch and broke his collarbone.

"You know, I could probably get two TVs for the same price if I just wait you out," Donna says and pries a bottle out of her housecoat. The pink fabric and orange furniture make my eyes burn. Cal is picking through Donna's underwear while she tries to twist off the childproof cap.

"You're talking about two hypothetical TVs there," I say. Hypothetical is a word the lawyer likes to drop in my lap whenever

I talk about getting the kids back. He says we'd have to start with some anger management classes, some group therapy—all the court-ordered treatments I've tried to ignore. Maybe I could get a few hours of supervised visitation if I followed those suggestions. The lawyer gave me the name of Cal's shrink, the same one writing prescriptions for half of Owen Sound and most of the reserves outside this town. We may be second cousins, but I know my brain isn't as mangled as that boy's mind.

"Hype-a-what?" Donna laughs, and slides an Oxy down her throat. She doesn't need to chase it with anything. Her lips are always wet.

"Hypothetical. Yeah, we might have to steal something else tomorrow, or someone will decide to toss their old set out for garbage day, but you're taking a risk there. We've got you a bird here, right in the hand. You can talk about the two you see out there in the bushes all you want, but they aren't sittin' in my backseat. Thing doesn't even have a serial number."

"Everything's got serial numbers in California," Cal says. His eyes have moved onto the VHS tapes stacked up by the busted old TV. Donna tapes all her performances at the Stockyard and tries to sell them on the Internet. Delaney's convinced her video is still a viable format. He needs the money, but can't afford a DVD player or any of that Blu-ray shit.

"No serial… Oh, hell no. You took the TV from the bar? Didn't Cal just start there? You really think Big Randy won't put that together? He's not stupid you know—just a pig. Just a rutting pig. He's all over the new girls now, taking them back to the office. Even when they gotta dance! Even when the crowd is rowdy, Randy's got 'em cooped up back there all for himself."

Donna and Alice used to be those girls back in the office with their razor blades and magic mirrors and stained panties landing on the floor. That's how Randy says it. Panties. He really liked to pop the 'p' between his lips and let the rest slip through his stubby teeth.

"So what if we did? He doesn't have any proof. There's no way he's letting the cops search the place, and there's no one bigger than Cal to stop us."

Donna taps her foot against the coffee table. Her frozen hair has melted and the couch is soaked behind her. She bites her purple lip and hums a little to herself. I know Alice it still sending her letters about Brad Paisley. About how soft his chest is in the night. About the booze and the coke and the taste of other men, how their sweat is cleaner, their minds are clearer. And I don't want to blame her, but I do.

"I dunno… two hundred for that shit? Really? Did you even grab the remote?"

Alice's old man shuts the door on me every time and her mother likes to call the cops to do spot checks on my place. Told them I was growing weed in the basement, that I had unregistered guns lingering around in the garage. Not a safe environment for children. She even told them about the stripper pole we had installed in the bedroom one Christmas, failing to inform the officers her daughter was the one who bought it in the first place. Everyone at the Stockyard called her Stacked Alice, even in toasts at our wedding. Her parents weren't invited.

"Alright—how 'bout this? I know you won't be findin' two TVs like this for Del anytime soon. And I know two hundred is a lot to part with. How about you give me one hundred for Cal and instead of my hundred, you just let me take a look at those letters Alice has been sending you from Florida."

Donna's wide eyes move from her toes to my face.

"I don't got any emails or letters, Jimmy. I told you. She isn't saying anything to me."

There is a yawn from down the hall. Cal keeps sorting through the videotapes, trying to line them up into alphabetical order. He likes to keep an order—a hierarchy of things. He includes women with those things, alongside ten-inch shrimp and thirty-two ounce steaks.

"Nothing? She's posting up pictures and all kinds of shit. She hasn't said a word to you? Bullshit, Donna. Just let me see a few and I'll just give you the fucking TV. You can have it."

Donna shakes her head.

"I'm not giving you anything, Jimmy. You understand a restraining order, right? You know she's not coming back until you're locked up. You get that?"

Alice's parents screen my calls. I don't bother leaving messages. Lawyer says that is just further evidence. Yesterday, I drove past the school a few times hoping to see one of them poke a head out of a window or something. I can't tell any of the kids apart in their snowsuits.

"I get a lot of shit, Donna. I fuckin' get enough shit."

I try calling the mill, try asking for a tour on the night crew. I can sling cases. I can use the forklifts. I know which trucks need a boost and where to find the temps taking another smoke behind the fuel shed. They tell me I'm suspended pending further review every time, like I can't read or something, like I can't see the notices lingering on my fridge, like Brad Paisley isn't playing in every single supermarket, singing about Alice in the mud, Alice in the backseat, Alice everywhere with him, everywhere but here.

I grab a bottle off the floor and chuck it at the wall. It shatters above Donna's head.

"Just show me the fucking letters, alright?"

Alice never liked country music. She used to make fun of the Hank Williams shit my Dad left me, rolled her eyes at all the Willie I played in the car. She called it my dead dog music. I slowly won her over, slowly watched her work Steve Earle into her sets down at the Stockyard, watched the men wince and moan while she took off her clothes. The words dripped off her with the sweat, and I knew she was coming home with me. It's always best to know.

It's the not knowing that brands you. Leaves a mark for everyone to see.

"Del! Del you gotta come in here now! You gotta get up! Fuckin' Jimmy—"

Donna is up off the couch and running down the stunted hall. There are only five rooms in this box and I can hear Del stumbling around in the bedroom, looking for the rifle his uncle gave him for protection after the cops confiscated everything. I grab another bottle of something from the sticky floor and chuck it down the hall after Donna. It catches her in the back. She falls onto the floor and the smell of gin fills my face. Not knowing is the worst part. Donna has all those letters with the details laid out in ink.

"Jimmy, there aren't any letters! There's nothing!"

Donna's looking up at me from the floor. I can hear Del stump toward me from the bedroom with one arm done up in plaster. The signatures on the cast are all his own. His ancient gun scrapes the wall as he moves. His tattoos are black and blue impressions of Donna's face.

No way will he buy that TV now.

"Get the fuck out of here, Jim," Del says. The floor is sticky. Cal tries to slip out the front door behind me with a handful of videotapes. Del is almost as tall as Cal. Used to toss dirt clods at his mom's car whenever she came to pick him up. Del liked to call her the town drain.

"Oh you brought the 'tard with you, eh? Doin' some community service tonight, Jim? He ain't taking any of those tapes with him, you know. Those are an investment. How you doin' anyway, Cali? You're momma ever end up taking you out there?"

Cal is tugging at my arm. He wants to go. He's forgot his postcards on the floor. According to the addresses, he's been all the way down to San Diego this week.

"You dumb fucks," Del says. "You think I wouldn't just jack the thing myself? I should just shoot you both down now, but no point there. With the injury, I might just get probation. Look at that poor 'tarded bastard. Why you gotta bring him, Jimmy?"

Everyone knows Cal was a mistake. Grew up with his mother and a bunch of rotating uncles, who left behind cigarette burns and the taste of soap in his mouth. Their cars stained the driveway until it looked like one big oil patch shining in the dark.

"We're going Del, alright? Just put your shit down. You don't need another violation."

Cal shakes his head. He doesn't want to put down Del's investment. I grab a few of the tapes from his giant hands. Cal's mother always told him his dad had run off to Sacramento, where he was doing play by play for the Kings on the radio. Del says the tapes are worth something, worth protecting, and Cal won't let them go. He needs the money for a ticket to the coast.

"Just give me the tapes. Give me all that shit and take your junk ass TV down to the pawn."

Cal starts chucking tapes at Del, just whipping them at the cast. One bounces off Del's face and spools of black tape sprout out across the floor. Little frames of naked Donna writhing on the pole unfurl across the sticky yellow carpeting. I can't see her face, but the outline looks like her. She's still crying on the floor, trying to avoid the broken glass. Cal hasn't been taking his meds for six hours now, and Del has been after him for seventeen years.

I watch Cal grab Del's broken arm and slam him against the wall. There is a snap.

"Put him down Cal, you gotta put him down," Donna screams.

The lawyer says the best thing for me right now is to stay out of trouble. Stay away from Alice's friends, her family. Stay away from everyone. I've spent too many nights inside, but I understand his point. Del is making some weird choking sound and his face is changing colours. I slowly back out the front door and let the screen shut quietly behind me. Donna yells something after me, something about calling off my fucking dog, but I don't got a leash. Cal won't need the money from the TV now.

The air outside is cold and the snowmen are still watching me. There's another bellow from the bungalow. Everything looks pink and grey. I put the car into reverse and pull out of the driveway. Cal is probably choking Del until he blacks out, the same strategy he's been using at the Stockyard for the last two weeks. You see the patrons walking around with purple throats the next morning, trying to order eggs through mangled voice boxes. Donna's probably flushing all their pills down the toilet 'cause the neighbours will be calling the cops again—a morning ritual in this neighbourhood. Sirens and birds to wake the children with the sun.

Brad Paisley is on the radio and his voice is singing to me about all little moments, all the dirty words. The time she lost the directions, and the time she burnt his birthday cake. He's singing about Alice and I know she's not coming back. I know there are no letters. The Panasonic is still in the backseat and it's watching me make a left onto a one-way street. One television is better than none, even without the remote. Only houses I've ever seen with two were in Cal's magazines and travel brochures. Palatial places down by the ocean. Places where the view goes on forever, a sight beyond your reach.

I need something I can't touch. Something my hands can't quite hold. Everything I cling to these days turns to shit and lead. Even the Panasonic is beginning to crack around the edges.

It's only twenty-five hundred miles until Modesto.

HATCHETMAN

DAD SAYS I'M NEVER SUPPOSED TO SHOW NO ONE THE TATTOO. THEY wanted my name to be Hatchetman on the birth certificate, but Grandma Hubert said no. She's dead now like the dog and the fish and all the other stuff that dies in our house. It was her house, but now it's our house. She couldn't say no no more. You can't say no to cancer, Mom says. You can't tell cancer to go nowhere. Mom says it goes wherever it damn pleases and sometimes I get scared it'll go for me next. People say I look the most like Grandma Hubert, even though I'm a boy. I think it's 'cause Mom shaves my head.

Dad's sayin' skin is stronger than paper, stronger than any bullshit certificate. He's sayin' skin is durable, skin is leather, skin is what they made Grandma Hubert's couches out of—animal skin but still. He's saying Hatchetman is a good name, a strong name, a name to be proud of and he's draggin' me into a truck we bought off of Sleepy, who's my uncle, but a fake uncle. He don't have any blood with me, and so he don't gotta worry 'bout the cancer like I do.

And we're in the truck with all the bottles from the rec centre we haven't returned yet and all the dead wasps in the bottles and all the half-dead wasps trying to crawl out of the bottles and Dad is sayin' skin is for life, skin is a pact. He says he's learned as much in twenty-six years on this earth. The stereo is the only new thing in the truck and it's playin' Dad's favourite Insane Clown Posse album, the one with the golden face on the front. I wanna pull over and pee, but the grass outside is long and yellow and filled with weeds. Dad holds my hand while he steers.

I'm lookin' for snakes in the ditches, tryin' not to think about peein' or Grandma Hubert or Uncle Sleepy and his two lazy eyes. I never wanna look at them, but it's like when you step on a bug—you got to look. And then Dad is sayin' how Grandma Hubert's final will was bullshit. But she wanted to live, I think. He's still mad that I look like her. He's still mad my name is Austin Saintclaire-Hubert on report cards, and doctor's notes, and detention slips. I never got to be called Hatchetman. He's mad, but he's holdin' my hand so I don't say she wanted to live. I nod and say yes, fuck Grandma Hubert and the dog and the fish and everything else that leaves me.

Dad is drivin' with one hand and we're off the good roads now, we're goin' to see Harmony, and we don't need a map because I been goin' here my whole life. All ten years. I remember the sounds of the needle and my Dad's back turnin' black like a cape and what cough syrup smells like. And then there is gravel under my feet and Dad's talkin' 'bout the Dark Carnival and a new album and he's so excited. He and Mom get so excited whenever ICP comes to town. They throw dishes and smoke in the bathroom and go see Harmony for days, but they can't now 'cause Grandma Hubert is fifty-six and dead and who's gonna watch me and little Hurley?

Harmony is Dad's best friend from way back in juvi, and he don't care that he's got a girl's name. He is sippin' Faygo he gets shipped in from Detroit, but it smells like he puts paint in it. He asks me if I ever heard of Johnny Cash, the first unofficial Juggalo, author of "A Boy Named Sue" and I say no and he laughs. I feel bad for the teeth he's got left. They gotta be lonely.

I was born a Juggalo and I will die a Juggalo, Mom says. I seen 'em throwin' dirt on grandma's Styrofoam coffin, I seen what dyin' is and I don't think it matters one way or 'nother if I'm a Juggalo or not. No matter how many times I paint my face or go to the Gàthering or get righteous with some mainstream faggots, I know I'll still end up in Styrofoam under all that dirt.

And Harmony says it's time for my first tattoo now that Grandma Hubert is gone—fuck that old cow, right Hatchetman? And no one calls me Austin at home, they all call me Hatchetman. I got named after the logo they put on all those Psychopathic Records—the logo you see tattooed on knuckles and tits and shoulders when summer comes around. That's their mascot—the Hatchetman. It's hot and Dad is lifting my shirt, but Harmony is pointing at my neck. How about there, right there, let's put it there instead. His lonely teeth shake when he laughs.

Skin is a pact. Blood is a pact. Me and little Hurley are in a pact for life and she's only five. She doesn't know about keggers or five AM police calls or what Mom's puke smells like. She doesn't know I'm here right now on Harmony's stupid porch. Only things she knows are she'll die if she eats peanut butter and Mom and Dad love to paint their faces on weekends.

Dad is sayin' I don't know, I don't know, and Harmony is laughing. We're on the porch and it's startin' to rain out there on all the yellow grass and the weeds and the hidden snakes. Come on, don't be a bitch, you hide your tatts at the factory, let the boy be a man. Let him be a real Hatchetman, a real psycho clown for once, and Dad is nodding okay, okay, go ahead and Harmony claps his hands together like thunder, but it's just rain out there.

The needle is sharp and hot on my neck and I'm not crying yet. I'm thinking about that dog and the fish and Grandma Hubert and what dirt tastes like. Dad is saying he doesn't like the blood, too much blood, and Harmony is singing his favourite ICP song under his breath. And I don't wanna feel the needle so I stay still and watch the rain outside the porch, watch the wasps drownin' in their bottles, the snakes suffocatin' in their ditches, all things just falling apart.

They're writing Hatchetman onto my neck in blue ink. I can feel the letters growin' and I don't wanna cry. They're on the letter "c" and the rain is still comin' down and I still gotta pee and Harmony is humming, humming out all the hate he has inside, and my Dad is smiling at me. He's smiling and he's so happy and I know my neck don't say Hatchetman. I know it don't say that. It can't. I can see it in his face.

Even dead Grandma Hubert knows all he's trying to say is "I love you."

THE LESSER HALF OF
SIR JOHN A. MACDONALD

GREG THE GOLDEN GOOSE NAMED THE FIRST LESION WINNIPEG. HE blamed that cold city for the illness that wracked his body now, the one that woke him up in the middle of the night screaming. It was the screaming that got him kicked out of the men's home the night before. He had lesions up and down both his arms like nodes on a map, crisscrossing veins, moles and scars from broken bottles. Calgary. Medicine Hat. Niagara Falls. Each lesion had a place these days.

He'd only ever been as east as Moncton, but that was far enough. He couldn't speak French and he didn't like the cops out there. They talked to you by looking you in the eye. They tried to act like a father figure, but all their kids were just as screwed up as anybody else's. They tried to call him Gregory. Greg had spat in one cop's face and spent the night getting beaten with a bar of soap. He would travel no further east than Montréal these days. The booze was cheaper there.

The line at the grocery store moved slowly. Greg clutched his last ten-dollar bill between two shaking fingers. He twirled it back and forth like a leaf. The Sun Chips in his other hand kept crackling every time he moved. Greg knew that the ridges on those chips would help them hold onto the inside of his stomach. He was tired of vomiting up all his food in tidy little piles in empty parks or dark corners in the shelters. He needed something with some texture, something with a little bit of grit to keep it down. Doritos hadn't done the job and he had given up on eating meat after two weeks in a slaughterhouse outside Hamilton. They had him push a broom to wipe up all the chin bristles from the pigs, bristles boiled off their snouts by the hot, high-pressured water. He could still hear the creatures grunting. They destroyed his love for bacon in that place. Greg would never forgive the slaughterhouse for that one. Sun Chips would have to do for now.

"Sir, this is the line for sixteen items or less. If you could go line up at another cashier…"

Winnipeg was still the worst though. The place was filled with tired faces and buses that couldn't make it two blocks without stalling. Your breath froze in the winter. You couldn't even piss yourself in the park without it freezing to your leg by morning. The summers were filled with mosquitoes and black flies, slowly turning your skin into one giant, red pulsing organ. They always seemed to go for the joints, the inside of elbows and the outsides of ankles and wrists. And there were always more to come. They would suck you dry if they could. The city tried to fight them off, spraying down the streets with trucks full of toxins. The first lesion was named Winnipeg, but he couldn't place all the blame on that place. It all went back to Jeremiah.

When it finally tore between Greg's fingers, the bill split down its length. The bottom half of its face fluttered to the floor. Greg watched it slide under a magazine rack decorated with wide blue-white smiles and horrible headlines about cellulite and murder and lesbian divorces. He could not pick it up now. The smaller, limp half of his ten-dollar bill stared back at him. The face was just eyes and the top of a nose now. It looked upset. Greg stuttered as the cashier gestured toward him. The yellow walls of the grocery store were pressed up tightly against him. The line of customers behind him seemed to stretch down all the aisles until all he saw was faces, sighing, angry faces gesturing for him to place his fucking Sun Chips on the belt so they could go home to warm beds and warm wives and all their whining children. The cashier rang his Sun Chips through and then stared at Greg's bent and twisted hands. The lesions hid under his long sleeves like the virus hiding inside his bloodstream. He held out what was left of Sir John A. Macdonald toward the cashier. She only shook her head. The man behind Greg coughed into his hand.

"We can't take that, sir. We can take debit and MasterCard. Do you have any change?"

Greg shook his head. He pulled the torn pink and purple bill back against his chest and walked toward the exit. The Sun Chips remained on the conveyor belt. No one followed him.

Winnipeg. Napanee. Hamilton. Fort McMurray. Nelson. All the named lesions and track marks on his arm hummed in the cold, but he was used to their bite. Greg the Golden Goose couldn't blame it all on Winnipeg. There had been the whorehouse in Saskatoon filled with American bush pilots and hunters. He had lost two teeth there, but they were molars, so it wasn't so bad. He had kept them in a jar until someone lifted his bag at a bus station in Oshawa. Another hole, another impression of an impression of Windsor, the hole of all holes, the hole eating through your arm and looking for light on the other side. Greg was never going back to Windsor either. There were also the Lebanese brothers in Hull who thought Greg could get them cheap E. They had held him in the back of a stretch Hummer until he bit one of them on the cheek. The man had tasted like Aqua Velva and had chased him for two hours before giving up. It wasn't all Winnipeg's fault. This whole country was letting him down on a daily basis.

Greg was the screaming man at the shelter now. He was the one who woke everyone up in the middle of the night, the one who got threatened with knives and bottles and a thick heavy hand shoved right up his ass if he didn't shut the fuck up. Greg wanted none of those things. He had worked very hard to avoid those things for the last five years on the road. So he was outside now and it was December, but still warm for December. December in Sioux Lookout was a different story—that was a place to go and die. Greg thought about doing that sometimes, just walking out into the snow and never coming back. Leaving behind all the Greyhound buses and the stupid CP trains. Letting nature run its course before whatever was inside his arms decided to make its final move. Sometimes Greg woke up and all he saw was light, but it was usually just a cop with a flashlight telling him to move along. All Greg did these days was fucking move, officer, but he complied. He was good at moving. He was getting better at complying.

The torn bill tried to escape from Greg's hand, but he clutched it tight against the wind. The Sun Chips probably wouldn't have stayed down anyway. They were related to Doritos in one way or another and the Doritos had been a disaster. The bathroom at Union Station had learned this the hard way, just like Greg usually did. He had determined this somewhere between Lethbridge and Regina after the frostbite took part of his thumb. He hadn't given that wound a name yet, but they were all connected anyway. You could follow the lines across his skin and they always connected with some gash, some hole, some new and spreading scab. Maybe he would keep fleeing until he hit Newfoundland and just skip New Brunswick altogether. He'd once bummed smokes off a Newfie who insisted on being called a Newfoundlander. The man even let him keep the lighter. If you held it right, the lady on it appeared naked. It couldn't be all that bad out there. Ontario had been a bust. Even the money here couldn't hold it together.

Sitting down on a bench in the park, Greg the Golden Goose held his damaged cash up to his eyes. The eyes of the former prime minister gazed back at him. They were asking a lot of questions. Why hadn't he shaved? Where was his hat? Did he know how cold it could get out here in December? Did he remember Confederation? Was he ever part of something from the beginning or had he always been one of those to bottom out on the end, to arrive just when everything was beginning to collapse?

Greg didn't have a lot of answers for the half-face staring back at him. He was too sober, too aware, too twisted by some strange pain in his spine, but yes, he had a beginning once. He didn't know where his hat was and he wasn't sure how cold it would get tonight, but Greg did know where all of this had started and it wasn't fucking Winnipeg, no matter how much he hated the smell of that place and the taste of its beer. It wasn't Saskatoon and it wasn't Hamilton either.

Splayed out on the park bench, Greg the Golden Goose remembered the pharmacy where they had hired him on after two years of college. It was just outside Surrey. It was quiet and it was mainly old folks with diet pills and cholesterol medication who came by on a weekly basis. They had a kid who rode around and dropped off medications. They had two women who ran the cash up front and a whole list of patients who kept dying off in their sleep. And then there was Jeremiah and his stupid hair and his stupid deal. It was easy enough at first, just slipping cold medication out during inventory, over ordering and underreporting. Most of the stuff wasn't even prescription. There was a new car and Jeremiah was always there for him. He was the one who called him the Golden Goose. Greg was the supplier. He was laying all these perfect eggs, and no one else had noticed.

So yes, half-face, he had been there for beginnings, for the great rise when everything looks like it makes sense, when all the pieces fit and everything is fresh and new and perfect. He had gathered hundreds of that face and so many others just like it and stacked them up in bank accounts and crammed them into a wallet too fat for his back pocket. He had to carry it in his jacket instead, had to swagger with the weight of all those full, fat faces in his pocket. Greg closed his eyes and blew a cold cloud out at the torn ten-dollar bill. He had been there for the fall too, been there to see how everything can fall apart just as fast. He was there from the start.

It was the kid with his bike who caught them slipping all those boxes out the back, the same kid some cops found in a river two weeks later with a Kmart shopping bag pulled over his head. And then suddenly the eggs were no longer golden and there was no more Jeremiah. There was just Greg the Golden Goose scurrying from place to place. Bank accounts were closed, cars were seized and property was claimed. Deals were made, and so Greg found himself fleeing from BC with a duffel bag and five hundred dollars. He found needles in Edmonton and flophouses on the border of Saskatchewan. He spent three days picking rocks before sunstroke took him out. He tumbled from place to place with eyes following him everywhere, asking about Jeremiah and the kid in the river, but he had no idea. He never asked for that. He just wanted to lay his fucking eggs filled with codeine and joy and fucking money. Jeremiah ended all of that.

Winnipeg throbbed on his forearm. He tried not to scratch the wound, but it was hard to keep his dirty fingers from probing the busted flesh. Everywhere he went, a new line was formed, hardening his arteries and weakening his veins until he had to poke at holes in his feet and armpits. London. Churchill. Kitchener. Thompson. Each one like another railway stop stretched across his body, whittling its way through his flesh until nothing else remained. Niagara Falls was right above his junk, a yellow pulsing thing he had been hesitant to name at first. The name fit now though—it was tacky and sticky and never seemed to stop leaking pus.

"I know all about beginnings, you asshole," Greg said aloud. He tossed the busted bill up into the air and waited for the wind to carry it away. The bill would end up in a sewer somewhere or in some bird's nest, covered in baby bird shit. Greg really wanted those Sun Chips when he thought about it. He needed something with some salt. The bill refused to disappear though and fluttered back down toward his feet. The eyes stared back up at him and did not blink.

"Alright, fine."

He tucked the bill back into his pocket and pulled a hood over his head. Greg still had no idea where his hat was—the half-faced bill was right about that one. Some asshole probably took it back at the shelter during all the screaming chaos the night before. He could feel the wind in his ears, carrying laughter from down the street. The bench was going to have to do for now. Winnipeg continued to throb on his forearm, but Greg the Golden Goose pushed away the pain. His veins would collapse eventually, but it didn't have to happen here.

This whole country had failed him, broken him slowly, but surely, into smaller and smaller pieces. His blood helped push the rot around, discovering new nerves to twist and muscles to paralyze. Greg would catch a train for Newfoundland tomorrow, until it ran out of track and he had to swim. He would find a bus or a car or whatever it took and then he would dive into the water. He would go to the very edge of this fucking country, and he would find an ocean there without any kids floating in its waves, their heads covered in plastic shopping bags.

He would just find water there.

The torn bill disagreed, but it was too late. It didn't have much say from deep inside Greg's pocket. The man from Newfoundland had said he'd wanted to secede, to escape all of this bullshit in Canada. That sounded alright with Greg. He bet they had cheap Sun Chips there too.

WRESTLING WITH JACOB

"YOU GAVE BIRTH TO MY COUNTRY AND MY PEOPLE. YOU KNOW THIS? Birthed them into this world, Rebecca. All of them."

The microwave read 2:45 AM. Five minutes fast. The man from the store sat at the kitchen table, his back facing the bedroom. The apartment door was bent and twisted behind him.

"I didn't mean to wake you, Rebecca. I'm sorry. I just could not sleep. There are so many words in my dreams. So cluttered. You know this word? Cluttered?"

Becca Crawford was familiar with this word. Her apartment was strewn with Darla's toys and clothing. Unfolded laundry and empty detergent bottles filled the living room. Her husband Terry had left all his baseball stuff behind jammed into the closets. All his old clothes smelled like dust and chalk. The shower drain was still clogged with his hair.

"What are you doing here Michael? You should—"

"Go home?" Michael said. His voice was wet. "Home where? Russia? Israel? No place."

Becca noticed the broken phone before him on the table. Moonlight caught the frayed wires, the empty plastic sheath and number keys scattered across a placemat.

"I don't go home, Becca. There is no home. That is a stupid word. I have a room, yes. Apartment, whatever. Not a home. You make a home though. You always have."

Becca had told the others at the bakery that Michael just needed a friend. He had no driver's license, no personal I.D. Just a flimsy passport from Russia, filled with half-completed travels. Always leaving, he had told her while trying to select a loaf of bread. Never returning. He had shown her the passport, filled with exit stamps, but no entries. His teeth were false and they clacked when he spoke. No returns.

"You were the mother of Jacob, did you know that Rebecca? All of us with these names, names from the Bible. You were the one who birthed Jacob and Esau. You know Jacob? Father of all the tribes? The one the angel renamed Israel after their fight. They wrestled for an entire night, Jacob and the angel battling with one another. Neither side could gain the upper hand. Always in the struggle. I should have been named Jacob, no? I should have been one."

Each morning he arrived with new purchases to display. Jim and Alicia tried to avoid the young man with the false teeth. He stared at your eyes when he spoke to you; he stared until you looked away and then he laughed. He brought all his purchases to the bakery to show them to Rebecca. New shoes and cellphones and TVs and the tattoo riding across the ridges of his back.

"Michael. You can't be here. You need to leave. We can talk about this later. Darla is still asleep and she has school tomorrow and I have to work. Don't you have to get up early?"

Becca didn't know what Michael did exactly. He never explained it very well. He paid in cash. His pockets were always filled with ticket stubs and receipts. He kept track of everything.

"For what? To see the sun? It will be the same as before. It is the one thing that does not change. Even the moon changes sometimes. Even the stars do. I should have been named Jacob."

Michael bought something from the bakery every day. Sometimes Becca saw him toss his sweet purchases in the trash as soon as he stepped outside the store. Jim told her it wasn't healthy, this fixation the man had. He looked young, still had pimples on his cheeks, but what was with the teeth? What was with that tattoo on his back, the dragons and the whores stamped onto his skin? Becca told Jim to mind his own goddamn business and stop touching her arm.

"Names can change. They aren't like the sun. You should not change yours though. We should all keep our Biblical names. Even in Israel, in the army, I kept mine. Rebecca, you should promise me you won't change your name. You should do this. Tell me you will not change."

Michael's thick fingers flicked a piece of the phone onto the tiles. Becca stood behind him. She could hear her daughter sleeping in the other room. A lonely picture magnet hung on the steel refrigerator with Terry's face staring out at the two figures in the kitchen. She forgot to take that one down after he moved back to South Carolina. She forgot to burn his clothes as well.

"Your daughter though, maybe you should change that name. What kind of name is Darla? Sounds like a whore's name, no? Sounds like it came from the Terry man. The baseball man."

It was Terry's aunt's name. The aunt who'd raised him after his mother got lymphoma and went on disability. Becca wanted to name their daughter Rachel, but Terry told her all about his years growing up with Aunt Darla. She drove him to all the tryouts, picked him up during rain delays and always had something to drink in the trunk of her car. At the funeral after her drunk driving accident, Terry had threatened to choke the pastor if he mentioned Darla's fondness for the bottle. That was a warning sign Becca decided to ignore; she stacked it beside all the others.

"Sometimes I think it was Michael who fought with Jacob. Do you know that story? I think I told you of their battle. Jacob was all alone. His mother Rebecca had died many years before. He was to become the next leader of the chosen people, to return his people to their land. He waited behind with his flocks and sent his family ahead one night. Before he lay down to sleep, he was faced with an unnamed opponent. A man with no name, like in a Western. Like your Eastwood. They wrestled against one another from dusk until the morning came. Each fought for the upper hand; each struggled to gain a foothold. I think of this on nights when I do not sleep. Some people claim it was a demon, of course, and not an angel. And maybe that makes more sense."

Another piece of the phone was tossed onto the floor. Becca leaned against the table and tried not to shake. Her heart rattled against her lungs. She should have listened to Jim and Alicia. Michael would not look her in the eye. Terry couldn't either once he told her he had to leave. She didn't stop him. She was tired of cleaning up his messes, filling out the forms for bail and paying the bar tabs down by the train station. Darla wouldn't even look him in the face. Terry was a third stringer for a minor league team, a bit of tangled hair circling the drain. He was hospital bills and dust and three beers ahead of everyone else in her life.

When she dropped him off at the bus station, Terry told her he would send money. He would send a cheque when he arrived and finally got settled coaching for some high school team. He had connections back home, people who owed his Aunt Darla a favour. Becca was still waiting for something to arrive in the mail. She still got his credit card statements. Bulk purchases at liquor warehouses and cigar shops. She ran them through the garbage disposal at the bakery. Becca didn't want to chance those fragments getting caught in the drains at home.

"And that makes sense, fighting with the demons. I do not sleep because I still see some faces. The ones we saw when they were blowing up roads. The ones who were children with grenades in their hands. I wrestle with their ghosts sometimes. I wrestle with children who have no eyes and who cannot speak. They hold my teeth, the ones their fathers knocked from my mouth in an alley. They hold all the fragments of their brothers that we left to rot in holes and pits and dark places. I wrestle with them because they have no souls. And they want mine."

Michael showed her his dog tags once. They said his last name was Luppa. He told her he survived the nights in rehab while his face was rebuilt by reading the Bible front to back. It was more exciting than he thought it would be. It was filled with battles and murders and children of children, a lineage stretching back to the beginning of time. It didn't all make sense of course. Michael did not understand why Samson's hair was so magical, or how Noah could build a boat so big. Michael said the New Testament was boring. Just the same story told four times and if Jesus could really raise the dead, he could have taken over the world without the Romans' help.

"But maybe it was an angel instead, yes? A test for Jacob to prove himself. I wish to have such a test, but there are no angels here. And so maybe it was the archangel Michael who wrestled him. The one from Revelations, the one who will lead heaven's forces against all the whores and dragons we have spawned from our cities and our dreams. I showed you the tattoo, yes? When it is finished, I want to believe all of this will make sense. They sent me here to be alone, to escape. I have done my service, but they still own something in my head, Rebecca."

"Michael, we can talk about this another time, okay? Please. I won't call the police."

"Why would you call the police?"

"Michael, look at my door. I can't go to bed with my door like that."

"Then I will stay. I will stay and watch the door. I am used to the night watch."

Michael's heavy hand wrapped itself around Becca's waist. She tried to pull away as he stood up from the table. Outside, the world was beginning to rupture around the edges. Pink bits of light bit away at the darkness. Michael's breath pushed itself into Becca's face.

"I showed you everything, didn't I? Do you think it's a coincidence we both spring from the Bible? You, a creator of nations, a mother to the father of the chosen people. And me, I could be that angel. I could be the one who gave Jacob his limp. The touch of my hand against his thigh ruined his leg forever. Did you know this? They taught us how to break a knee in training. How to break it firmly, how to break a leg so they will never be able to run from you again."

Up close, Becca could see the scars running down Michael's chin. That was where the shrapnel hit him, he had told her at the bakery. He took her hand and made her feel his skin.

"I know how to break a bone."

"I know you do, Michael. You told me. You told me."

He released her arm and sat back down at the kitchen table. Becca wanted to run, but she remembered Darla's chest rising and falling in the other room. The neighbours here were all asleep or working the night shift. This was a building where the elevator always smelt like piss and dogs were tied up on balconies. Terry was gone and no one from work could call this place.

"Why did you take apart the phone?"

Michael flicked at the numbers. He didn't answer her. Becca stepped back behind the counter toward her bedroom. She was too nice. Terry had barely paid rent during the five years they were together. Becca always gave the regulars extra frosting on their Danishes; she never argued with a work schedule that saw her rising at 5:00 AM to board a bus across the city while Jim and Alicia slept in until seven. She did not jaywalk at empty intersections, but instead waited until the light decided to change. The world was already chaotic enough, filled with Michaels and Terrys and all that revelation. She didn't want a hand in the chaos. She was afraid she might lose it in the process.

"They use phones to make us die. You know this though. Like I told you. They will not face you like the angel. They will wait until you are in range, and they will blow off half your face so you can't recognize yourself. They will make sure you are not the same. If you cannot touch them, you cannot assert your dominance. They will take your teeth and cast their spells and you will be left on that strip shuddering. I shuddered. That word. I did that until some-one dragged me away. A phone is for those who can't stare their enemies in the face, for those who want to listen, to speak without betraying their face.

"You can lie over a phone. You can tell me this makes sense. You can tell me I should go home. A Christian in Israel, still a Jew in Russia. I am homeless like all those sick and dying dogs in Moscow. The ones who ride the subway as if they are people because they do not know themselves. I clatter around my own tongue."

Becca continued to back toward her bedroom. She watched Michael remove his shirt, the black lines of his tattoo rippling with the effort. He tossed it onto the floor beside the fragments of the phone. His voice continued speaking. Becca paused before step-ping into her bedroom.

"You gave birth to all of this, and I wrestle with the demons you left behind. I find them lurking everywhere, even in your bak-ery. I see them snickering behind us and I know you cannot hold a secret. I thought maybe you could help me rebuild things. They could only help me with my face. You told me of your Terry and your Darla, and I knew you could do better. I knew you could find better names. We are all wrestling through the night, and in the morning, some of us lose. Some of us awaken without a friend on a mattress in the dark. And it is always so dark."

Terry was the religious one, if you could call it that. He called it the last resort. One night he sat where Michael was now and told Becca he could never be a true believer, but the science was just too depressing. Terry did not like to check his stats, his on-base percentage or his fielding numbers. He despised the breakdown of his sport into columns and lines and algorithms. Not because they were wrong or misguided; they were all too accurate in fact. Terry couldn't bear to see all of it laid out before him. He could not watch his thoughts, his dreams, all of it, reduced to chemical reactions. Terry told Becca he did not want a world where every cell was just slowly unspooling toward its own end. This biological pre-destination was just as bad as all those evangelicals preaching their guaranteed promises of redemption. All this decay was purchased in advance and Terry was tired of being confronted with the best before date.

"I followed you here, but I did not think I would come in. I am not usually such a rude houseguest. But I am tired of this haunting, Rebecca. I am tired of trying to make all my friends from scratch. They want me to go back to Israel. They want me to sneak off with them in the night, to use my new face, the one no one will recognize. I am wires and wet work now. I read those words about wrestling with Jacob, and I am always that angel who is losing. I am the one who must rename him, who must surrender part of myself. I am that demon or whatever it was that found him alone amongst the sheep. I need you to make me new."

Becca disagreed with Terry. She watched his career spiral ever downward, his numbers declining while his waistband expanded. She watched his confidence crumble, the easy grounders slipping through his legs, the fly balls lost to the sun or to his hangover. She could not allow for some grand mystery to conceal the facts, to deny the reality she faced every day. The science inside the bakery was not a mystery, the science was sound and it was repeated daily. It was not all death and destruction. It was new and well-crafted and reusable. Terry told her all things had to end and he preferred not to see them coming. He left her at the bus station with a cross hanging around her neck. Bits of his chest hair clung to the chain.

"You need me here, Rebecca. You can help me create something new, just like your Darla."

Darla did not talk much about her father. She was only four. She liked to play with the pieces he left behind. The well-worn baseballs and chipped bats he kept in the closets. They did not fit into his luggage. Becca stepped back into her bedroom and fumbled through the dark.

"We will have to start the world over, Rebecca. This is what I realized today. I realized it when you told me you didn't know where to turn anymore. You told me you did not want things to stay the same. I can change all these things. Do not think anything of these problems though. Even the whores in the Bible, they are all eventually redeemed. Even Mary Magdalene."

The bat was chipped at its tip. It was heavy in her hands. Michael still sat facing the busted door. His hands covered his face as if he were weeping, but there was no sound. A knife lay beside the phone on the table. The apartment was filled with pink light. The tattoo on his back featured a seven-headed dragon with a woman on its back. It rippled as Michael spoke through false teeth and stitched lips. It seemed to enunciate his words.

"You gave birth to a nation, to all the tribes, and I know you can do it again, Rebecca. We can do it again. I just need to show you how it is done. I will show you one way or another."

Becca crossed herself and swung. She still believed in physics.

THAW

I HAVE TWO FINGERS LODGED IN BIG DAVE'S RIGHT CHEEK WHEN HIS fat fist connects with my left eye socket. The world is made of gin and pain and salt as I hit the ground amongst the snow. Blood is spat onto my face and some of the townie girls are giggling, but they don't move to lift me up. I can hear Tanya in there somewhere, her voice hitching itself to the tumour in her throat, the one the doctor's called benign and circled in red marker on her scans.

This is the third weekend in a row; the third time I've stumbled out behind the Trap with hands balled up into fists and tonic on my tongue. I can already hear the siren again, but for once I'm the one on the ground and there is a weight on my chest. It joins forces with some other pain and presses down onto each rib, reminding my lungs of their limits. Big Dave kneels down over my face and his thin blood drips down into my eye. He is silent, except for the hoarse cough rattling his chest. I think about diseases, the viruses coursing through his veins, the smell of his two kids covered in their own shit down at the welfare office. His wife lost custody a few weeks ago. Big Dave rolls back off my chest, and I gasp for breath as one more fist connects with my teeth. I underestimated his rage, the hate boiling in his rounded gut. Women's voices scatter as a flashlight reveals their bundled faces to the dark.

"Get offa him. Now. Get. All of you. Get. Go home."

Red and blue lights go on and off, but the edge of my vision only sees snow and broken bottles. Bottle caps and cardboard support my back as I try to piece together what my face must look like now. Probably like the two boys I clashed with last weekend, the ones who asked for their mothers while their girlfriends fled screaming for non-existent bouncers and help, help from anyone who would listen. I ruined my new winter coat with the splashback from their pimpled faces. I got locked up for a few days after that one. I have a lot of fines to pay.

The Trap stands on the edge of town, the end of one long road with two stoplights and no crosswalks. There are dead dogs under the snow that we will find in May once all the ice recedes back toward the lake. There are teeth and fleshy bits of ears and gums beneath the frost, pieces put there by men like me and some of the natives who fall asleep while trying to walk home after the bar has closed. The government ships us body bags at a discount in the spring once the snow starts to disappear. Lately, I've been sleeping with the Zamboni at the arena, letting it thrum against my chest when I wake in the morning, scabs and fluids dripping from my face like fleshy post-it notes from the night before.

"Chuck, get the fuck up. Get your ass up. You dumb shit, up. Up!"

Mitch is staring down at me. The collar of his uniform chafes his neck and I can see where the razor must have skid across his Adam's apple this morning. He yanks me up by the hood of my coat and the cold bracelets embrace my wrists one by one. Mitch boots me in the tailbone like he used to when we were kids, and I land on my face. Cuffed on the ground, I realize I can't stand up. The snow tastes like old beer and smoke.

"Good job, Mitchell. Good fucking job. Are you going to help me up or am I going to sit here all night? Davey got his blood all over my face. I think it's freezing to my skin."

Maybe it was just something with Big Dave's face. A long face filled with baby teeth and a fat tongue always hanging from one side of his mouth. The kind of face that leers in its sleep, scoping out whatever ass walks into its dreams, following women into bathrooms, listening to their private sounds through the door. Maybe Tanya just laughed at one of his jokes. I don't need many reasons right now. I press my tongue against loose teeth and then Mitch hauls me off the ground again and starts dragging me toward his cruiser. A few onlookers snap pictures with their phones. Big Dave is gone by now, humped shoulders lurching toward his basement apartment and the mangy cat he keeps on a leash in the summer. A replacement for his kids.

"Third weekend in a row now, Chuck? Shit, you smell like the fucking recycling bin. Always back at the fucking Trap. You could just stay home, you know? Drink in the dark like the rest of us do. Now stop dragging your fucking feet and get in the goddamn car."

The Trap has had a lot of different names. For the last few months, it has been the High Table. Before that it was the Sparrow's Nest. Donnelly's. The Roost. Number 7. The Hole. None of them last though. The bartenders remain the same, sneaking bottles out the backdoor, halving their prices out there in the tiny parking lot. Only the owners change, dumping their investments and fleeing back down to Thunder Bay or Toronto or wherever fleets of snowplows wait for intermittent storms. I'm on call for the plow up here. We only have one.

The car door slams behind me. The heater in Mitch's cruiser is still broken. He's yelling at the group gathered around the Trap, the one leering at my busted face and the red impressions I left scattered around the dumpster. We all started calling it the Trap back in high school when the first place burned down, filled with a touring group of strippers and their drunken admirers. The local rag told us all about the screams and the underwear seared like a second skin to fleshy forms identified with dental records and skin samples. They flew a plane in with the families from Quebec and South Dakota to make identifications on some of the victims. Mitch and Jake and I walked through the wreckage on our

Christmas break, fascinated by the lonely chrome pole still held upright in its centre. No one dared to lick it in the dark.

"Can't you do something productive, Chuck? Get a dog or some shit."

Mitch turns off his flashers and we begin cruising down the strip. There is no snow tonight. I am prepared for another night in a cell away from photo albums, high school yearbooks and old letters. I am ready for a night without my shoelaces.

"Where's your good old partner Gordo?" I ask, and kick at Mitch's seat.

"Quit that shit, Chuck. Gord's got appendicitis or whatever he made up this week. He's at home. He's warm. He's a dick."

"So my suspicions are confirmed."

"Shut up, Chuck. Take a look at your face."

I can see a ridge of purple over my eyebrow in the rear-view mirror. There are long brown lines down my cheek where Big Dave's blood has begun to dry. Outside the car, we pull past the police station. It looks like a high school portable with a few stranded Christmas lights affixed to the roof. Soon the street-lights begin to disappear and homes dissolve into shacks and sheds. Mitch switches to his high beams. We are the only car on the road.

"Uh, buddy, where are we going? I'm bleeding from the head here."

"You know it'll probably be charges this time? After those two kids last week, it'll probably be charges. Three weeks in a row. I talked to Tanya, and she says you keep calling too. Calling at five, six in the morning. Calling and hanging up. People have call display, you know that, right Chuck? People got jobs to go to in the morning. Three weeks buddy. Just go talk to her."

The trees reach up to block out the sky and the paving turns to gravel. I feel each stone rattling my bones as I bob up and down in the backseat.

"I don't call anybody…"

Jake was the one who got out. Got the grades, the placements, the money. Mitch and I lingered behind, sticking with what we knew. Jake was the one who had us sneak out into the dark and stare at that pole, looking for leftover wallets and cases of rum that hadn't exploded in the flames. The Trap always called him back for the holidays, an institution that never wavered in the cold. Always rebuilding, always rebranding; never changing at its core.

Jake was the one who tied himself on skis to the back of cars, the one who climbed trees for the sole purpose of jumping back down from their branches. He liked to run naked in the snow.

"We're going to the lake," Mitch says. He won't look at me in the rear-view and I don't blame him. The ice out there before us glows along its blunt and ragged edges. Mitch and I had both stuck around town once all the exams and track meets and bullshit house parties ended, just like Tanya did. She didn't want to follow her brother anywhere. She told me she liked the cold. She liked being able to sit in total darkness. She said that's where you find exactly what you needed. I agreed because I wanted to see her again.

I agreed because it sounded stupid and I didn't know what else to say.

"Just take me to the station, Mitch. I know it'll be charges or court or whatever. I don't care. Pile it on. It's cold out here. Your shift ends in like, what, two hours?"

Jake was back to celebrate that the tumour was benign. It was a faulty killer, a failed revolution against the state of Tanya's body. There would be no surgery, no radiation, no wisps of hair lingering in every sink and bathtub in her wake. There were drinks and piles of wings and the smell of pork trapped in the air that night. As it got darker, Mitch clocked in across town for his shift while Jake and I argued over snowmobiles. Tanya watched from the window as we revved engines in the dark and headed out into the snow. November was supposed to be cold enough, but lakes aren't arenas. They hold cracks and crevices, clutching lives and smaller things in stasis. They rupture like bodies do, like teenage faces in the dark. They crumple and swallow, but rarely spit things back up. Not until they are ready. Not until they decide it's time.

"I said you can just take me back to the station, Mitch. I don't fucking care. Maybe it'll get me some more time off. Just have one of the other guys deal with me. One from down south, one of the boys who can't get his car started in the morning. Come on. This is stupid."

The funeral was quiet with an empty casket. No one pounded at their breast. No one pointed fingers in my direction. I sat in the front row, but I didn't move. I never heard him tumble through the ice. I didn't look back to see him fall. Once I circled around, the hole was too wide. The water was black and nothing glowed under the surface. I felt it splitting like a quake behind me as I drove away, unable to lift anything out of the water, unable to recover the body.

"We are going to the lake. You know Big Dave will forget he destroyed you by the time he wakes up tomorrow anyway," Mitch says. "We'll keep you off the books for now. I know you'll be out there next week anyway, looking for more black eyes or whatever you're trying to fucking collect. I won't always be the one who drags you off them. Eventually, some idiot is going to go head first into a window or a wall and then you will be gone too. But you fucking know that, don't you Chuck? Of course you do."

Mitch shuts down the car and leans back against the cage. He would have been out there with us on the ice. We found one bottle of rum in the wreckage of the Trap years ago. Jake had us agree to drink the whole thing together. Mitch's eyes are tired and his thin lips don't open very wide. The flaps on his hat make him look like a dog, one that's been kicked too many times.

"I'm going to go for a walk. Can you sit tight for an hour?"

"It's freezing out here, Mitch."

"I know."

The door slams and I watch him walk down to the shoreline and out of view. The car is parked near the frozen water and I can hear the wind rushing across its surface, scattering the windshield with pine needles and flakes of snow. The cuffs around my wrist are still cold. All I can see is this white expanse through the glass and the view goes on forever.

I try to roll onto my back. Someone has carved the word BACON into the left door with the edge of their cuffs. I kick at the seat in front of me and decide to close my eyes.

No one was able to pull the body out. The frost closed up the ice. The cracks were too long and wide for anyone to get too close. Jake floated somewhere under the surface, his helmet embalming all the screams I imagined for him, the ones flooding his lungs with froth and tiny waterborne bacteria. The snowmobile was down there too, a rumbling anchor filled with gasoline. Rough estimates were made for spring retrieval. More body bags were ordered. Nights at home became ordeals and so nights out became a makeshift solution. A new path that somehow always led toward the Trap, toward that metal spire they kept like a monument in the centre of the dance floor. There's no space for spires out here on the ice—it cracks and rebuilds with each fluctuation in the weather, reuniting former pieces into new, less familiar wholes.

I open my eyes. I wait for Mitch to return and undo my cuffs. My face has been reshaped each night by someone else's fists. My knuckles have split and reknit themselves repeatedly in return. They look old and undone by the constant cold. Skin flakes and peels while I sleep. Blood reroutes itself around busted capillaries, detours around holes punched through my skin by rings and nails and the sharp edge of a beer bottle. All of this will heal, but none of it will remain unchanged. I can hear the blood moving through my face as I exhale another cloud.

Tanya said the worst part about the hospital was the constant light, the alarm clocks stuck on midnight and the endless flashing beepers. With all that light, she couldn't sleep. I told her that I understood, even after the tests came back clean. I told her that it all made sense. She wanted the darkness, the kind you find up here when all the stars have fled. Out there beneath the ice, the darkness swaddles everything. She says that's where you find what you need, once all the other stuff is stripped away, once all these old distractions are finally removed. After the moon disappears and the steam of your breath evaporates, there is only you out there in the void.

I sit waiting for the lake to thaw and I want to believe her.

TOWERS

WHEN THE PIT FIRST OPENED UP, THE CITY SAID THEY WOULD COME out and fix it. Kids tossed pop cans down its maw, waiting to hear them clink. Some of the older tenants whispered that there was no bottom to the hole. I watched its edges spread, swallowing the courtyard that used to stand between the four apartment towers they built to keep us from messing up their city streets. So many people out here got needs and wants displayed openly on veiny arms and pitted faces. They call it Willow Ridge, but nobody could mistake this place for a golf club.

"Alice, I don't want to see those dishes in the sink when I get home. You hear me?"

Dad moved out here when the plant shut down. They were making tricycles until someone sued and the whole thing closed up shop. I was still in diapers, but I remember a house somewhere on a street full of golden retrievers and Dalmatians. I remember a mother and the sound of bikes ringing their bells. I remember grass that had yet to die and trees swaying in a yard. I don't hold these things against him. I tell myself they are dreams. I know dreams always have a lie buried in them somewhere, up to its neck in all the things we wish were true and all the things we don't want to say. I bet those dogs got rabies.

"I hear you. The dishes. Got it."

"I mean it this time, Alice."

The door slams and I can hear him pounding down the hall-way toward the elevators. Only two of them work these days. The super says it's too expensive to fix the other ones. Dad would take the stairs, but we're on the twenty-sixth floor and his heart isn't the greatest. Sometimes he gets winded walking down the hall-way with the groceries. Sometimes he falls asleep on the toilet and I consider going in the kitchen sink. I don't like to wake him up. The dishes in the kitchen now are a few weeks old, but they can wait a bit longer. I'm used to the smell.

I turn off the TV and walk over to the window. Down in the courtyard, police tape flops back and forth in the wind around the pit. It's so dark down there, sometimes you wish there was no bottom. You might just fall forever from one side of the earth to the other, exploding on impact with a star out there in the galaxy. But I know it's just a sinkhole, slowly expanding around its edges. One day one of the towers will topple inside, but the city says that's a long way off. They don't have anywhere else to move all the people anyway. They keep hoping some of the poorer ones will die off.

"Did he leave yet?"

Kayla just walks in because she's Kayla and her mom can't spell manners or anything else. She comes to stand beside me at the window, looking down at the pit. She smells like plastic fruit and those flowers made of paper at the Chinese restaurant down the road.

"I heard some of the boys threw a dog down there, and you could hear it yelping for like five days afterward. They felt bad by the third day, but what could they do about it, you know?"

"Your mom tell you that?" I say, pressing my nose on the glass.

"My mom would believe it, I'm sure. She's conked out in bed if you wanna go to my place to escape all the dude smells. You know your dad could at least wash his underwear in the sink or something. Or just burn it. I'd prefer that smell."

Kayla's dad lives in one of the other towers. Even though they are only five minutes apart, she doesn't see him much. A lot of people get lost in the buildings out here. We don't even have names for them. North, south, east and west—no one's got the energy to be more creative. Our parking garages are filled with forgotten jet skis and boats from when people thought Willow Ridge was going to be something. They had brochures and everything. There are still a few floating around the lobby with big pink font and black and white pictures of appliances.

"Alright, so what are we doing? You going to get Tyler to come over again? I know you think he digs me, but the lazy eye just ruins it every time."

"Nah, we'll see him tonight," Kayla says. Her teeth are too straight for these towers. The older men like to whistle at her from their balconies. Sometimes they toss garbage at us if they are drunk. The janitors the city sends out here every few days push most of the trash down into the pit. One day, we might fill that hole all the way to the top.

"I don't wanna stand outside in the cold tonight, pretending to enjoy beer," I say. We are headed down the stairs now, stepping over sticky spots on the concrete.

"You don't need to pretend, you just need to drink more. My mom says you can take some of her schnapps if you want, but not to drink it all. She needs a reason to get up in the morning."

Kayla only lives one floor under me. Her mom used to be the guard the city hired to watch over the pit, making sure no one fell into it. Eventually they eliminated the position and just posted signs warning that the municipality would not be held liable for any accident involving the "temporary" sinkhole. They added the police tape for flare I guess. Kayla's mom didn't handle it very well. She figured the pit was going to be there forever. There was no need for a back-up plan at the time. The safety vest she wore still hangs in their living room like it's a homemade quilt or something. The blocked font reads PIT GUARDIAN.

"So you're sure she's asleep?" I ask, before flopping down onto the orange couch.

"Zoned out, more like it, but that's about as close as she gets. You take what you can."

At two in the afternoon, the towers are quiet. Summer means all our fellow teenagers are at home, hanging out in the parking garages to escape the heat, smoking up whatever they can grow in closets full of rigged lamps and heated blankets, waiting to sell their homemade wares to kids from the suburbs. Willow Ridge is full of clogged bathtubs and empty cold medicine packages. Sometimes you find them in your mail.

There are stains all over the couch, but I try to ignore them. Some things just don't wash out. Kayla pulls two bottles out of the kitchen and plunks them down on the coffee table. The glass is smeared with powder and too many fingerprints. The TV is sputtering on and off, but we aren't really paying attention. Most people only get the same six channels. The satellite companies got tired of tenants tearing their dishes off the roof. Henry Gosling on the thirty-second floor thinks the government is after his brain. He's tried to cover all the elevators in tinfoil a couple times, but the other tenants peel it off before he can really prove anything about brainwaves or conspiracies. I want to believe him. Staring down at the pit would make a lot more sense if there was a reason behind it, if we could blame it on someone in the shadows.

Otherwise, it might just be a hole.

"So what's supposed to happen tonight?"

Kayla is still in the kitchen. She doesn't like to eat in front of people.

"I don't know. Tyler and the Chads said we should just meet them down there after it gets dark. They said they'd clear out the scabs before things get too crazy. It gets hot up here anyway. Heat rising, all that bull. I just don't wanna listen to them talking about tits again like we aren't sitting right there. At least pretend, you know?"

The TV features people screaming, but they don't really mean it. The tendons in their necks aren't straining and their world is filled with unchipped furniture and well-organized magazines. I can't find the remote and I don't want to stick my hand between the couch cushions. I imagine something moist and warm hiding underneath them, waiting for my touch. Something lonely.

"You wanna bet it's just going to be those three idiots tossing bottles down the pit? Maybe they'll decide you should go in next. Don't you get tired of them?"

Kayla shrugs and sits down beside me. She pulls her hair back behind her head. Kayla's got a hole in her ear where one of her mom's piercings turned all infected. The doctors cauterized the hole so it wouldn't spread. Cauterized is the longest word Kayla knows how to spell. She likes to show off the medical report. She says it was an experimental procedure, one of many. I don't know what else has been done to her. There are injection sites like crop circles up and down her back. When she takes off her shirt, it looks like she's been branded.

A fist pounds on Kayla's door, but neither of us get up from the couch. We can hear him wheezing in the hallway. Arnold always knocks before pushing himself through the door; it's the closest he can come to being civil. His gut swings before him, filled with deep-fried everything. Arnold keeps the water running through this place, fixing the clogged toilets and broken water mains that make everything feel damp to the touch. He's like a super who doesn't get paid. I hold my breath as Arnold lumbers past us toward the bedroom. His hair hangs down his back in one, long ponytail. It's got bright red elastics woven into the greasy mess. Onions and yellow stains follow in his wake. He doesn't bother to say hello. Kayla looks down at the rippled carpet until we hear her mom's bedroom door slam. The drywall is thin.

"Wake up, Ginny. Wake your goddamn ass up."

Before the floor can begin to shake, before another repetition of their daily ritual can begin, Kayla hurries out and down the hallway. I'm forced to chase after her toward an elevator, past empty units filled with busted televisions and those polyester bears you win at county fairs. They're blue and pink and rotting. Kayla climbs into a shuddering box, and I know we'll ride the elevator until she feels better, until the sound of all those pulleys and winches tells us this place is anything but real.

Tyler's grandma claims his lazy eye came from too many days staring down into the pit after they moved him out here during the fifth grade. He's been out here almost as long as me. I don't know what he saw down there. His grandma says it's like staring at an eclipse for too long—staring down into all that darkness, staring into something that doesn't end. She says it does something to your soul, but that's usually after she's taken too much oxygen and Tyler has to wheel her back into the windowless room where she sleeps and draws on the walls. They give her chalk and magic markers. She seems happy enough if you don't look too close.

"You need to get a monocle or something, Ty. Just to balance your face out. How 'bout it?"

There are floodlights down in the courtyard. They spin our shadows in every direction like we aren't sure where to go. Occasionally, cigarette ash flutters down around us from the balconies above. You have to avoid the hot ones. I undo my hair and watch the Chads harassing Ty. They're supposed to be identical twins, according to their mother, but one is a foot taller than the other. They both have orange hair and chase rats in the north tower until the little creatures' hearts explode. The bigger Chad has bed bug bites up and down his arms. He tries to tell me they're just ingrown hairs. I don't know why the little one has been spared.

"I can see fine guys, it's only the skin around the eye. Hold still and I'll show you."

Kayla and I are perched on a bench beside an old refrigerator. The door is down at the bottom of the pit somewhere, probably still full of old salad dressings and leftovers. The beer the boys brought is warm and attracts little swarms of gnats under the light. They drown by the dozens in the half-empty bottles we've scattered in the weeds. Old paving stones and bits of porcelain hide in between dandelions. We watch Tyler pitch his bottle at the smaller Chad, who tries to catch it between his hands before it explodes at his feet. The spray makes it look like he pissed himself.

"If you had an eye like mine, you might have caught that."

"Suck it. You owe me a beer now. I bought that shit."

"You stole it," Ty says as he tosses a paving stone over the yellow police tape and down into the black of the pit. "Go home and get a new pair of pants."

"It's too far."

The pit has spread slowly since I was a kid. It started out more like a well. People used to poke poles down there. My dad said it spread while we slept, waiting for everyone to look away. Like a pot of water waiting to boil, except nothing was overflowing, just sinking and draining. Now you have to walk around it to get to the other towers. It adds ten minutes to each commute from one tower to the other. I don't even know if a Frisbee can make it across.

I like to run my hand along the temporary poles and police tape they got set up along the edges. The maintenance guys gave up on barbed wires fences after the pit swallowed the third set in a row one summer, after Dad got hired at the chicken feed place. It makes all his clothes smell like rancid butter. They have him running back and forth with bags of corn like he isn't fifty-five years old, like his back isn't made of glass and string and chalky bones. His tendons are all coming undone in the middle of the night. I can hear them popping on and off with the radiator.

"Move your skinny ass over, Allie. You should be nicer to me."

Tyler sits down beside me on the bench they've got here to commemorate Kayla's mother. She saved me once from falling in when I was five, but my name isn't on the plaque. I am referred to as "the child." I am sketched in bronze and I'm smiling. Tyler's lazy eye bobs up and down beside me. I place a hand on his leg to stop him from shaking. I don't even know what colour his eye is today. It fluctuates with the weather like it can't decide who he wants to be.

"I am nice. I don't call you the half-cooked Cyclops. I don't call you Hawkeye or Lumpy. I could be meaner if you like, but I think you should just get used to this nice me. This is as good as she gets. Sorry to disappoint you. Well, not sorry, but you know."

"Probably the nicest thing you've ever said to me, either way. As nice as you get, anyway."

I don't remember why I ran toward the edge of that hole. This was before Kayla started going for all those medical tests, paying rent with injections and taking the new treatments for food allergies—providing solutions for all those parents who still can't handle the fact that all our air has been recycled since the start of time. Kayla's mom spotted me hurtling toward the ledge in my yellow footie pyjamas. No one ever explained how I got down there by myself. Apparently she caught me just at the edge, before I discovered what lay down there at the bottom. There was an article on the front page of the paper, back when Willow Ridge was in the news for more than the occasional assault charge or string of petty thefts. Kayla says her mom still has a drawer of those newspapers bound up in butcher twine under the sink, going yellow along the edges where mice come to nibble and spit up the mess. Our faces are coming apart.

The Chads are dragging a case of empties toward the edge of the pit. Ty jumps up to join them and Kayla just shakes her head. Big Chad keeps telling her she can sleep at his place, and I'm afraid she might just agree. I don't blame her, I guess, but I don't want to imagine Big Chad's tiny little tongue licking her spine.

"He always tells me you're like him. You wanted to go in. Sometimes Mom gets up outta the bed and all she talks about is chasing after the little yellow rabbit. You were the only one she ever caught, you know that? The rest came out here at night and climbed the old fences. They came when no one else was watching, dropping like rain with no one listening."

Kayla pauses and passes me another beer. Its bubbles spurt onto my hands, but I don't wipe it away. I let it linger and wait for the bugs. At the edge, Ty and Big Chad swing the case back and forth between them. A few lonely ashes flutter down from the balconies. You can hear someone weeping through an open window. Big Chad releases his end of the case and lets it fly, but Tyler keeps a firm grip, like he's going to pull it back up all by himself. Little Chad is the only one who screams. Kayla clutches my arm until the blood stops flowing, but she doesn't say anything. I find my tongue is trapped between my teeth. Little Chad screams again, but Ty has already toppled over. Big Chad is on his knees at the edge, staring down into the black, calling for Tyler. The pit swallows each echo. Another empty can clatters down from the west tower. It bounces off the dead grass and rolls toward the edge, but doesn't fall—as if it had a choice in the matter, as if it could decide.

"You can't let it keep you up all night," Dad says. He's busy putting on his shoes, tying laces that will come undone before he reaches the elevator. They've got him on the night shift now, clearing out clogged receptacles and chutes in the belly of the factory. The grains roost in his wrinkles. He's always covered in mealy dust. Only the rain washes it away.

"I'll sleep when I want to, alright? You're the one who sits in the living room all day instead of using an actual bed."

"It's bad for my back," he says. "You try climbing stairs at fifty. School starts back up in like a week. You need to get back on a schedule."

The police only came out after Tyler's grandma threatened to call the paper and the local TV lady who needs to touch up her roots. People fall down there all the time, the officers said. There is visible, posted signage. It is a well-documented hazard. People approach it at their own risk. Compliance is too expensive to enforce. One of them said it would be like guarding every beach up and down the coast. The Chads stopped talking to me and Kayla after the officers questioned them for two hours in the basement of the north tower. The officers asked me if I had been intimate with Tyler. I asked them if that meant I slept with him. They just jotted down my response and said they would look into it.

Memorials at Willow Ridge don't last long. Flowers and wreathes disappear in the middle of the night. Some tenants blame it on the pit, as if it's got the power to drag down all our reminders, to make us forget what's happened. Dad closes the door quietly behind him. He didn't say much about Tyler falling in—he only asked if it was the kid with the lazy eye, who kept coming by our place to ask if I was home.

"So I can come out now?" Kayla says. She crawls out from where she's been hiding under my bed all day. Arnold has moved into their place downstairs. He fills the fridge with whole chickens and the cheaper parts of pigs, frying their feet up on the stove. Kayla says the whole place smells like toilet water now, forever gushing down her throat when she tries to breathe. Her mother tore down the PIT GUARDIAN vest from the wall after she found out about Tyler. Kayla is wearing it underneath her coat, even though it's warm out. I pull a backpack onto my shoulders.

"He won't be back for like ten hours."

Outside, the pit waits. The towers only make it look deeper. You can hear dogs crying from the bottom, coyotes that got lost looking for cats to snatch in the middle of the night. They have joined the bottles and the burnt couches. The spires are waiting to collapse. I can hear them trembling down to the foundation as we ride the elevator toward the ground. We've got a rope made out of bed sheets and some food and enough flashlights for three people. The pipes and wires in this place are unravelling, decomposing faster than the remaining residents, faster than we can descend. Outside, gnats are hovering above the surface, hovering above the trash and the curses and everything else we've thrown down there. Soon the towers will fall too. We have fed this hole long enough. This sinkhole was a warning: all things must come to an end eventually, little yellow rabbit. All things must come to a close. Even at five years old, I knew that.

Kayla and I just want to get there before everybody else.

MUTATIONS

"HOW MANY TIMES DO I HAVE TO EXPLAIN THIS TO YOU? ALRIGHT, number one: I don't even work inside the plant. Can you get that through your head and then listen to me for one second?"

Janet is tossing cutlery into a big black garbage bag in the kitchen. Forks and knives are poking out of the bag, but she doesn't notice. She pretends not hear me over the noise outside. Mrs. Gibbons is mowing the grass. Ever since her husband left her two years ago, she's been doing all the household chores and going to yoga twice a week.

"Number two: I don't even go inside there to go the bathroom. They've got this Porta-Potty set up, so I don't have to duck inside the building if you don't want me to, you know? I can just stand…"

Janet has moved onto plates now. Not the fancy wedding china. She took that in the third load last week. One of the old plates misses the bag and shatters across the floor. The motor outside cuts out and I can hear Mrs. Gibbons singing an Old Spice jingle to herself.

"If all you have to talk about today is Porta-Pottys Luke, I'm sorry, but I don't have time to listen. I don't want to hear about the brochures either. What you need to do is pretty simple at this point. No one would hold it against you."

Each word is terse. We've rehearsed this over and over the last six months. Ever since the Coopers' baby was born with a third ear growing out of his left cheek. The doctors at the hospital said it was fully functional and otherwise perfectly formed. Cooper's been in charge of reactor maintenance ever since I started at the plant. All I do is check their IDs at the gate. Six hundred feet from the nearest building, eight hundred from the closest reactor.

"I'm just trying to explain. Like I said before, they've got some real precautions in place, but everyone is just overreacting. Just because he works in the plant doesn't really mean much, you know? We've got all this new kind of mixed concrete and you should see some of the stuff they've been doing on the inside…"

Janet slams another cupboard door. Dust is floating around us in the kitchen. It sits in a thin layer all around the house. She took all the cleaning supplies to her mother's place in the second load. I don't mind the dust so much. It reminds me where to put things.

"Alright, well how about this?" I say. "I read it the other day, at work, you know. They've got these girls down in South America, and they're born, seriously, with legs fused together like mermaids. And they've got these Chinese babies in some mining town coming out with their eyes all covered up with calcium scales. And no one really knows why, you know? No definitive causes. Just genetics. You know how much of that stuff can go wrong. So I think you're really just jumping to some pretty bizarre conclusions here, instead of weighing, you know, the facts."

Another cupboard slams. Janet turns to face me. She's got dust in her hair. Outside, the mower fires up again and sputters.

"I don't need to hear any more of this Luke. You know I don't. I'm tired. Tired of your excuse, and your three titanium barriers, and your two hundred feet of concrete, or whatever you want to believe. It's all just numbers to me and guess what, Luke? I'm tired, like I said. I'm scared. I'm tired and I'm scared and I'm not going to stay here. You can come with me. I would like you to, but I know I can't make you. I am going though. And no one is keeping you here."

Janet walks across the kitchen, dragging garbage bags behind her. The sun catches the dust spinning in galaxies between us before she slams the door. I don't say anything. Outside the mower roars and the starlings in the old pines whine for their mothers. I look at my watch as Janet's car pulls out of the driveway. I need to get to work.

I lean on the glass in the security booth and frown at the greasy mark my forehead leaves behind. Someone has been playing hangman with Post-it notes on the day shift. All the answers are dick jokes. Caplansky and Gerry are getting bored again.

"My dick is so big it graduated high school three years before I did."

A sedan pulls up to the window of the booth, and I recognize Larkin's wrinkled face.

"Same shit, same shit?"

"Pretty sure that's not how it goes, Luke."

"You get the sentiment," I say.

"After today, yeah."

I haven't seen Janet in two weeks, ever since all the inside employees started getting tested for radiation before and after they show up at the plant. Everything is low profile. No one wants to scare the herd and have property values plummet. No Hazmat suits. No clunky vans with onsite analysis. No lab coats. Just freshly pressed three-piece suits, blood tests, and urine cups.

"I'd just like to piss into something bigger than a coffee cup, you know?" Larkin says.

"Yeah, I hear you. Once you start, it's hard to stop."

"And the thing's at most maybe a medium. Shit."

"Oh yeah, that's gotta burn if you're running on a full tank," I yawn.

"I'll see you tomorrow. Maybe they'll have a bigger cup."

There have been two more babies in the last month. Larkin's sister-in-law ended up with a kid with a tail. Not just a few extra bones, an actual tail. Doctor said if he cut it off the kid might never walk normally. Throw off his balance. Never drive, never play sports. At least this is what I'm told by the maintenance guy at the hot dog truck on break. They named the kid Evan.

The Tierney household only has to deal with two belly buttons on their newborn daughter. Side by side. Her name is Julia. All of this could be bullshit of course. Last summer, we convinced Adam Caplansky that there were teeth at the back of the vagina. A whole set, like the ones in a shark's mouth. He believed us for a couple of weeks before his girlfriend found out.

Still, both fathers are on the inside of the plant doing whatever it is their salaries require. Tierney and Larkin's brothers work deep inside. Out in the booth I know I've got some barriers in the way. I trust in what I can touch. Lead paint, titanium alloys, concrete barriers, monthly safety audits. Run your fingers over the digits and smell the metal in the air.

On the ride home, I notice For Sale signs that have sprung up along my street. Word gets around. The blinds at Mrs. Gibbons' place leer open at me as the car bounces into the gravel driveway. The crabgrass I fought all summer is curling up in yellow and brown splotches on the lawn. Mrs. Gibbons has been dumping flyers for spiritual counsellors and emotional audits into my mailbox each day since Janet left with both our crock-pots and half the bath towels.

I open the door to the house, whistling for the cat. I never gave him a name. Growing up on a farm, I learned how foolish naming an animal could be. A calf steps into the wrong patch of ice and he's gone. No Suckles or Jerome or Judith the Wise. Just a frozen side of beef, floating with its eyes open and unblinking under the ice. Wait until summer before you can pull it out safely.

I set the mail on the counter. Janet has been by again. She only stops in while I'm out now, slowly emptying her closet. The last few shirts lingering are stained with lime green paint from our kitchen reno. She's grabbed most of her stuff, but she still sends these pictures. Postcards. Postcards I guess 'cause she started mailing them. We've stopped arguing. Her mother always denies she's home, and I know Janet doesn't want me driving over there. Last week I drove halfway and then turned back. Six hours wasted in the rain. The phone remained silent at home. No messages.

Instead of phone calls, I find these photos in the mailbox like postcards from Janet's own personal apocalypse or something. Three-headed toads from the Amazon where Chevron's been digging. Six-legged wolves stalking the ghostlands of Chernobyl. Indian children blind from birth, eyelids stretched taut over their sockets. African albinos butchered by tribal leaders for medicinal purposes. Most of the photos are grainy black-and-whites, like she's pulled them from the tabloids. No words on the back. Just pictures. I know what they are saying. It does not take a thousand words. Leave. Find me. Come home. Be safe.

I feed the cat that has grown fat in Janet's absence. I still make too much breakfast in the mornings. I plop myself down on the couch in front of the TV. All the shades are pulled down. On the screen, Godzilla battles Hedorah over a miniature city, flames raining down on the citizens. With drooping eyelids, I listen to the crackling screen for Janet's voice to make its way through the static. The television is muted. Outside, Mrs. Gibbons drops something in my mailbox and the starlings cackle.

The first doctor we went to said it might have been my sperm's motility. I had to ask what that meant. Movement and speed apparently. I remember Janet staring at me like it was my fault.

The second doctor said Janet might be suffering from polycystic ovarian syndrome. She just glared at him, thin fingers smoothing invisible wrinkles on her lap over and over. I made sure to write that one down so I'd be able to repeat it next time her mother called. There was a history of it in her family, according to the doctor. Her mother called two days later to tell Janet all about her new niece, Ellen, six pounds, four ounces. Perfectly healthy and coming home in just a few days. I went out and bought the cat that afternoon.

The third doctor told us to just keep trying. He handed a prescription for steroids to Janet, and checked me on the spot to make sure I wasn't wearing tighty-whities. Those things work like a pressure cooker on your swimmers. He told us not to worry. I went through a regimen of cold showers and avoided drinking after work. Janet bought a calendar and started plotting out her cycle. She gave up smoking and started chewing gum. None of it worked. None of it helped. And a cat is just a cat.

Old soy milk bottles fill the overstuffed garbage can in the booth. I try holding my breath while scouring the *Reader's Digest* for typos. The day shift must be on a health kick again. Two months ago it was bananas. Larkin pulls up to the gate. His face is thinner.

"No more piss taking?" I ask.

"Nah, we all checked out fine, Luke. People are always overreacting."

"With two tails, they wouldn't be swimming much anyway, would they?"

"Yeah really, I know, right?" Larkin says.

"So no more pissing in your coffee cup?"

"No, that's over, thank God. Office was beginning to smell. Later buddy."

In "Laughter Is the Best Medicine," I find an "allgator" instead of alligator. I circle it in red pen and try to draw one in the margins.

The baby with the tail died in the hospital. The funeral was a mess of cameras and Larkin's brother ended up charged with aggravated assault after he decked a photographer with the priest's lectern. No press or protestors dare to come around here. I wouldn't be able to do much even if they did. I can't really run anymore, and I left that off my paperwork. Management never bothered to follow up on it.

When I was eleven, a bull shattered my foot. I went inside the barn to feed the heifers after dark. Dad had forgotten to lock him up. I just remember the smell of manure and a crack that traveled up my spine and exploded somewhere in my brain. They found me in shock on the floor half an hour later. My mother had to cut my boot off to bring down the swelling. Everything smelled like manure for weeks after. The bone never really knit itself back together like the doctor said it would. I can't even handle stairs very well anymore.

I lock the gate to go on break. Even now, visitors are scared to go near the Larkin family. One of the maintenance guys tells me he's heard about how contagious this stuff has become. The mother's bedridden, the older kids experiencing growth spurts in all the wrong directions. Talking bent dicks and ballooning eye sockets, man. He grins at me from under a mangy three-day beard like a stray that needs a good kick. He drenches everything in mustard. Even relatives are mailing their condolences, he says. The postman leaves them at the very lip of the driveway, a surgeon's mask tied over his face. Florists refuse delivery. The maintenance guy bites into his sausage, mustard seeping into his moustache. He grins at me. I dump onions all over my hot dog and walk away down to the water.

I should be back in the booth. Rearranging pens or leaving some Polack jokes for the day shift to read in the morning. Maybe leave them the answers too. Caplansky usually needs that extra push to get the punch line.

"Why did the Polack cross the road?"

"He couldn't get his dick out of the chicken."

There are fences down by the bay. I walk along the chain link and toss my tinfoil wrapper into the water. Sludgy waves smack against the heavy rocks they've lined the shore with to prevent erosion. Someone has cut a hole into the chain link. Kids used to come down here years ago to jump off the rocks until one cracked his head open on the way down. That's why they hired me. I crouch and push my way through to the other side. The rocks are soaked. I sit down on the wet edge and stare into the water. I try to breathe and my mouth fills with rot. On the rock surface the algae seem to glow a sickly purple. I slide my feet down towards the water, heavy steel toes dangling into the muck. I look for a reflection. My feet are getting wet around the edges. Around me, the algae have lodged themselves. The fence is covered in small patches of it, like fur. I dip my feet all the way into the water. The cold seizes them. Closing my eyes, I imagine the purple working its way into my shoe, into my socks, into my flesh. Re-knitting. The cold clenches my feet hard; the water pushes deeper in between the cracks. Rebuilding.

I shake my head and pull my feet up. Violet algae cling to the laces and squirm their way into the eyeholes. I scrape each boot off against the fence and worm my way back through the gap. I don't bother marking the hole in the fence down in my logbook. No one comes around here anymore. Not even the safety inspectors.

Back in the booth, I circle "asociate" on the contents page. I let my foot throb in rhythm with my pulse. I stick my head out of the booth to breathe in the air. My lungs fill with a sickly sweet smell rolling off the bay. The humps of the plant stare back and, in the breeze, they tremble.

Mrs. Gibbons is sitting on my porch when I get home. The fluorescent light makes her hair look dull. She smiles, but keeps her teeth behind her lips. The cat's in her lap, licking her hands.

"What is this?"

She waves a photograph in my direction as I step out of the car. An ultrasound of a baby with four arms flaps in her hand. Find me. Come home.

"Who would leave this in a mailbox, Lucas? Is everything okay with Janet?"

I yank open the front door and flick on the light. The plate Janet smashed still sits on the floor swept up in a corner. I pull myself a glass of water from the tap.

"What does it look like to you?"

She dangles the picture far from her face like it's rotting.

"Is she pregnant, Lucas? Is this hers? Is that why you kicked her out?"

"I didn't kick anybody out and no one is pregnant. Jesus. You know she left on her own. She'll come back here when she's ready. When she realizes it's safe. And it is safe. I don't even work inside there. You know that. Shit, it's safe inside too. All of this shit over nothing."

The cat purrs against Mrs. Gibbons' breasts. Her dress is a dark red spattered with flecks of dishwater. She isn't wearing a bra and she's shaking the ultrasound in her hand. Another postcard. Her nails look all chewed up.

"Mine didn't come back. Jack left and I'm the one carrying the debt. The man had more credit cards than brain cells. He's gone now. New name, new life, new wife, I'm sure, 'til he gets bored again. Not that I blame him now. It looks like everyone is leaving. They're not even waiting for a sale anymore. And now we've got people leaving, well, this... stuff in our mailboxes?"

"One baby with a tail and the whole neighbourhood goes apocalyptic. They'll all come back when they realize how much money they're throwing away. Wait and see."

I turn on the television. Flicking through the channels, I find a baseball game I can ignore. The score is 13-3. You don't come back from something like that.

Mrs. Gibbons leans in the doorway.

"Why don't you just go? I mean, a job is a job, but you can't really be expected to stay..."

I yank off my work boot and chuck it into the corner. I peel off the sock. Badly knit bone pushes at the skin around my ankle and the top of my foot. The old root is what Janet called it. Mrs. Gibbons takes a strong interest in the ball game as I massage the scar tissue. My sock still smells like algae. Most of my toenails flaked off years ago.

"I'm surprised they let me keep this job, honestly. First chance I have to run after somebody, they'll have me inside stamping paperwork and sorting out the mail. It's not like they do a physical or anything. We're basically rent-a-cops, not marines. I don't even get pepper spray."

Mrs. Gibbons sits down on the floor by my busted foot. She doesn't say anything, just lays a hand on the jutting ankle bone and turns her eyes to the screen.

"Plus, when you think about it, I turn and run, what's that say? I know how safe the plant is, I know the codes, I've seen the blueprints, you know? We print all that shit in the brochures, and it's no joke. We aren't some crazy Russians translating an owner's manual for the fifteenth time from Greek or something. I might not know how the atoms divide or how they harness all that power exactly, but I know what I can see. And I see half the seaboard lit up every night without fail. I see safety measures put in place, physical precautions put in place. I'm not relying on some divine intervention to save me because I can see these things. Know them. Confront them daily."

Mrs. Gibbons doesn't reply, so I show her all the photos. The abnormal and the broken things Janet discovers each week in the tabloids. Mrs. Gibbons spreads them out across the floor. She counts them, loses count, counts them again. Sixty-three photographs, each cut like a postcard. I lie on the couch with the television muted while she tells me about her husband. About the gun collection in the basement. The nephew he'd slapped at her family reunion. The bouts of erectile dysfunction. The videotapes he stashed under the mattress to give his future son. To teach him how to be a man.

"I made sure to burn all of those. Not that we had a boy. Just the principle, you know?"

Around the ninth inning she begins to drift off. Janet never could fall asleep before me. She liked to watch me, she said. Another home run and there are fireworks on the screen: 14–3. I stare at my foot, waiting for it to glow purple, for the cracks to fill up again like they did out there in the water. The fireworks dissipate. The crowd cheers. I wait to be whole again. Another player steps up to the plate, but the game is already settled.

Mrs. Gibbons is asleep on the floor with Janet's photographs sprawled around her when I wake up. The clock reads noon. On the television, baseball has given away to a monster movie marathon. I watch Ebirah battle with Godzilla in the ocean, green blood swirling around the specks of people floundering in the water. I always liked monster movies. You know where you stand with someone like King Kong. He can't escape, can't hide, can't linger in your water supply waiting for you to brush your teeth. King Kong can't sneak up on anybody.

Outside the door, I can hear the cat mewling to get back inside.

When I was a kid, my friend Chuck Borden snuck a snake into our tent at camp. Wrapped up in my sleeping bag, I lay awake convinced every shifting blade of grass was that garter. Holding my breath, I lay parsing out the seconds 'til the inevitable bite came. I lay that way throughout the night, listening to the rise and fall of little chests for a hiss or slither to alert me. Every sound was a forked tongue probing my ear. In the morning, I found the snake in an old margarine container. Chuck had forgotten to poke air holes in the lid. I still prefer the bull in the pen.

The cat continues to whine outside. I pull myself off the couch, one boot still on my left foot. Mrs. Gibbons has used my coat for a pillow on the floor. I watch Godzilla falter as the sea monster gains the upper hand and muted foreign faces scream in horror. Mrs. Gibbons stretches out in her wrinkled dress and yawns.

Whenever a mouse got inside, it was Janet who tracked it down with the frying pan or the pizza slicer. I stayed off the floor until she gave me the all clear to come back down off the counter. She was the one willing to reach behind the fridge and pull it out by the tail and toss it into the yard. Or crush it under her shoe and throw it into the trash—still breathing.

I yank open the door. In its mouth, the cat carries a baby bird. Mrs. Gibbons mumbles behind me, clutching the photographs from Janet to her chest. The cyclops antelope. The three-tailed possum. I carry the ultrasound image in my hand, fingers crushing the four-armed wonder into a ball. A doctor's address is scrawled on the back. Janet always had terrible handwriting.

Three titanium alloy barriers and two hundred feet of concrete.

The cat drops the bird out of its mouth. Pink and downy. It stares up at me with three purple distended eyes the size of marbles. The cat cocks its head at me and turns to go back outside. I follow his tail out to my car. The hood is splattered with little bodies glowing pink under the sun. I look up and wait to hear their mothers. The cat leaps up onto the hood and begins nudging the bodies with his nose. The birds don't recognize their babies anymore. The trees remain quiet. The nests are empty. I push the cat off the car and start to sweep away the little pink splatters.

I still have to get to work.

SUCTION

AFTER THE THIRD PAIR OF HEADLIGHTS SWERVES TO AVOID US, I ASK Last Call Paul to pull over. He doesn't look at me, just presses his foot down harder. Snow lashes through cracked windows and seeps down into the collar of my jacket. Each drop slides down my spine. I rub my back against the threadbare seat. Last Call just can't stop talking.

"My daughter, you've met her, haven't ya? Donna? She's a good girl you know, a really good girl, just confused. Teenagers, you know? You should know anyway. How old are you? She's just in a place right now where—well, have you ever tried training dogs?"

Staying with Paul wasn't my first choice. After eating Tom's last box of Cap'n Crunch and hanging up on his mother for three days straight, he tore up the rental agreement we'd made out over a pitcher at Le Sketch a few months before and flushed it down the toilet. I had never bothered to make photocopies. My stuff was stacked neatly on the curb afterward.

"That sounds bad, doesn't it? I'm not calling her a bitch, you know. That's not what I'm about as a father. Her mother, though? Well, let's not open up that can of shit. It'll just ruin the night. Suffer to say—suffice—suffice to say, she's a fucking whack job. I'm talking three rubber walls and a locked door. You know what I mean?"

"Four."

"What?"

"Four walls, Paul. You want four walls—Jesus, stay in the lane!"

Another pair of headlights swerves onto the shoulder and Paul is just staring at me.

"Usually pick her up from school every Friday. But I go there this week, and she's not around. First thing I think is, oh no, something's happened, 'cause she's got the diabetes, like I told you before, ever since she was a little girl, you know. Real bad, too, like real bad. No cake, no nothing. Not fun for a girl growing up, but she always, well, she always took it in stride. Very resilient, Donna is. Anyway, first thing I'm thinking—"

"You're thinking she's gone to the hospital," I say and snatch the beer bottle off the floor.

"Exactly. Exactamundo, my man. And as a father—well, shit— one word for that. Terrifying. Absolutely terrifying as the most god awful shit you could imagine."

The sign for Millbrook pops up. Ten kilometres. Paul swerves across the line, but there are no headlights in sight. I am imagining too much right now. Severed arms, blown kneecaps, Last Call Paul's head in my lap just talking endlessly into the night while I wait for an ambulance that never comes. Somehow, my imagination has decided it's worse if I live.

"So, I call up her mother, and the fucking electrician answers the phone, the one I told you about at lunch? Yeah, he answers the phone like he lives there, meanwhile, my name, my fucking name, is still on the lease. And he's answering the phone like he of all people is man of the house. And it is my phone, did I tell you that?"

"Like everything else in the house," I mumble.

"Damn straight. So we get talking, and no she's not at the hospital. No, she's not at work, and no, she isn't with Louise. So where is she? With a boy maybe? Well, Mr. Sparky says, how am I supposed to know? Can you believe that?"

A transport is leaning on the horn and snow is piling up on the windshield. Last Call's heater has been out for weeks. I only know because he bitches about it every day during lunch while we play euchre for pennies in the break room. Sweet Pete, Joco, Larry B—all those guys have already put me up for a few weeks on their couch or in a back room or in a shed with a space heater. Whatever they could do until their wife or dad or girlfriend or girlfriend's dad caught me jacking food from the fridge and clothes from the hamper.

All my stuff is now in black garbage bags in the trunk.

The transport hits the horn again, and Paul throws his eyes back on the road. His glasses are fogging up, but he doesn't care. He's set on beating closing at Hilda's Bar and Grill. It's just down the street from his apartment. A walk-up apartment, but a nice walk-up. Second floor over some Hungarian deli. They give him a discount on peameal bacon on Sundays.

"So, now I've got a Friday to myself. No idea where Donna is, but hey, that's going to happen sometimes, no big deal, no big deal, not like we don't see each other. But we don't anymore. We don't see each other. It used to be that we could just hang out all the time. Watch the ball game. Maybe work on the yard, the flowers, whatever. She even just liked doing the vacuuming, you know? Loved it, just fucking loved it as a little kid. Could barely hold the thing. Pulling it all back together was the best part, you know. And now? Nothing."

I scrunch myself lower in my seat, realizing if we do crash, I will probably lose both eyes to shattered glass, both knees to the glove box, and most of my hair in the ensuing fire.

"So I just kind of sit there in the school parking lot. It starts getting dark, so I call the house again. Louise picks up, says she's not sure, but she'll have Donna call me right away when she gets in, and that it was very sweet of me to worry. And it's, well, like this real civil sort of conversation for a few moments and then we both hung up. Just like that, like none of this shit ever happened. Some actual civil human interaction for once. Unbelievable."

Buildings begin to pop up in our headlights. I can see the sign for the bar still sputtering in between the snow. I push my fingers out of my sleeves and run them along the dashboard. Ice is forming around the lock on the glove box. Bottles and old vhs cases rattle around my feet as Paul turns into the parking lot. He's no longer talking, just sort of panting. I almost can't see his eyes, which are probably red and purple blotches behind his fogged glasses. He runs a hand through his hair and belches into his palms.

"This is the place, my friend, the place."

I whack the slush off my boots at the door and hear cheers as Paul sways inside. A couple of regulars in knit caps and old Oilers jackets sit trading stories at the bar, half empty pints growing warm. A line of scraggily booths, duct tape holding in their deflated stuffing, separate the bar from the dining area. A few regulars stare at the bubbles moving ever upward through their pints. The bartender waves at Paul and marks another line on a chalkboard behind the taps.

"Fifteen days straight now, Paul? A new record!"

I nod at the bartender and order a gin and tonic. Paul keeps yakking to him about the management and the new contract for unloading the trucks. I collapse in a booth and crush the ice in my drink between my teeth. The bar is wallpapered with a flower print like my Nana's place. Paul sits staring at three pints in front of him. He smiles. One of his canines is missing. Down the bar, the two guys in Oiler jackets compete with the television volume.

Last Call Paul always worked the afternoon shift. Getting off after midnight, he made sure to make the rounds at the bars around the warehouse before coming home. Half-lit neon signs, orange pool tables, places with only three brews on tap. Temporary homes, like way stations on the hazy odyssey home. Sleeping on the couch became a comfortable position for Paul, until one night when Louise decided to keep the couch and everything else, according to her attorney and the family court. She packed all his stuff up in garbage bags while he was at work. He told me he lost half his records when the dump truck came by in the morning.

After a two-week suspension for dropping a forktruck off the loading bay dock, Paul came back into work a couple months ago. I smelled him before I heard him behind me in the locker room. I stood there in my stained underwear while he told me about his weekend.

He'd gone over for Donna's birthday, without any cake, of course, her being diabetic and all. He and Louise were getting along 'til he found a hammer under the couch. He didn't own any Mastercraft hammers, he told me. Never bought his stuff at Sears like some of the other guys he knew. Never trusted the place after some blonde nancy had screwed up the alterations on the suit he wore to his Dad's funeral. Everyone could see his ankles the whole ceremony. And maybe, yeah, maybe he'd had a few too many, but it was his daughter's birthday, can't he celebrate that? Louise was talking on the phone to who knows who, and it was his goddamn house. Donna wasn't even paying attention; she had some movie on the television. Some bullshit with Demi Moore, except she had a boy's haircut.

And all Last Call Paul had? Well, all they'd left him was this hammer.

"This bitch ralphs on the deck we built," the one Oiler bellows. "Anyway, she comes back in to grab the vacuum cleaner, I guess to clean up her gunk, and turns it on before she gets outside. Full blast. The dogs freak, just freak like mad and start shitting all over the carpet."

An antique armoire from Louise's grandma, a handful of porcelain penguins, three window panes, and five thousand dollars in damage to the kitchen later, Last Call found himself with a restraining order and three hundred hours of community service—picking garbage off the road.

"So now we've got dogs shitting all into the old shag carpet in front of the TV," the Oiler laughs. "Sheila's waving around this Hoover like she's going to shoot up the dining room…"

"Hoovers ain't shit, man," Last Call says. "Let me tell you as one man to another: Hoovers ain't shit. What your old lady needs to get is a goddamn Dyson. Now that's the kind of shit you need for a vacuum. That shit's got suction, it'll pull out all that shit stuck in your stain."

Last Call is all up in their faces now, his arms draped around the two Oilers fans at the bar. I'm waiting for a fist and a scream and snow filling up my body cavities as we wait for the ambulance to arrive. None of this happens. It isn't as bad as being in his car.

"Why, haha, oh man, Last Call you alright? Why not a Hoover?"

"Well, see the Hoover," Last Call says, "Well first of all, J. Edgar Hoover? Asshole. So there is your first problem, am I right? Second off, you gotta look at manoeuvrability. Like, sure suction is a big deal to some, but if you can't get in the corners, or 'round the furniture, you're going to have a pretty dusty place, right? And another thing, it's too loud! You want a thrum, not a hiss when you're trying to clean shit up. That hiss will haunt your dreams otherwise, and your paycheque too, 'cause those sons of bitches break down more than Oprah."

The two Oilers nod, smiles creeping across their faces.

"How you know all this shit, Paul? You selling for them on the side?"

"Oh yeah, I'm selling for all those big suits now," Last Call says. "Bissell, Kirby, Oreck, Kenmore, Panasonic. A Hoover machine, in my humble estimation, is just not worth the investment. You gotta know your machines. Gotta put a premium on suction."

The bartender shouts out last call. Paul waves him off.

"How do you do that, eh Paul?" the one Oiler says. "What's the secret?"

"Well, it's a trade secret for me, you know? You gotta hold 'em, feel the vibe they give you. That's how you know. Just put a hand on them. They'll let you know. A lot like dogs that way."

"Oh, really?"

"No, you dumb shits," Last Call roars. "I'm just fuckin' with you. You gullible bitches."

Paul staggers away and waves a hand at me. He's supporting himself against the door frame. I pull myself up out of the booth, a lone strip of duct tape tethered to the back of my jeans. Paul slams the glass doors open and I pull my coat tight against the chill. As soon as he's out the door, the two Oilers start sniggering, slapping each other's backs and imitating vacuum sounds.

I follow Paul down the street into an alcove beside the Hungarian deli. Tomorrow is Toonie Tuesday for shaved salami. Someone has spray painted RUCKUS in black across the door to Paul's apartment. The streetlight in front of his place is busted, so we stand in the teal and pink illumination of the deli sign. Snowflakes pop and hiss when they touch it.

"Finally got the little bitch into the hole. It sticks sometimes."

I follow Paul up the stairs, stumbling around piles of cleaning supplies, dragging my sleeping bag behind me. I leave the garbage bags in the trunk to freeze overnight.

"So, like I was telling you before, about Donna, you remember, right?" Last Call says.

"You ever find out what happened?"

He opens the door to the apartment.

"Well, like, she calls me up later that night. Here, just toss your stuff on the end table. You can use the couch there. She calls me up and we start talking. Turns out she was volunteering that day down at the old folk's home near our old house. Well, my old house. I don't know."

I try lying down on the couch. It's covered in sweaters and blankets. The whole place smells like stale beer and sweat seeping into the drywall. The kitchen is stacked with old beer bottles.

"What don't you know?"

Paul pulls off his shirt and rubs his stretch-marked belly. Purples lines crisscross his chest.

"Well, it's kinda fucked man, ya think? She'd rather spend her time with some old fogies, slobbering all over themselves and trying to eat the Monopoly pieces during game hour than hang out with her Dad? Not like I was going to take her back to this dump. I know a dump when I live in one, alright? But she'd rather hang out with them for four hours than go bowling with me, or whatever? I mean, at least I can feed myself."

Paul turns off the lights in the kitchen. He opens up a closet and starts yanking out spools and spools of electrical cord. As I unpack my stuff, I watch him line them up against the walls. I don't say anything as he carries two vacuums into his bedroom.

I try to close my eyes and hear Paul bump into the television. The volume is low and a sports reel is playing. He's shoving vacuum plugs into all the open sockets, even unplugging some lamps and an old answering machine to plug some more. He turns each one on as he goes, the sound building like a swarm across the floorboards. He runs a few more cables under his bedroom door and they tangle together in the thick, pink carpet.

"But Donna, she'd rather be working in a place like that, for free. Volunteering," Last Call says. "She says it's for school, but why not work at a summer camp or some shit, you know? Go pick trash on the highway with your old man. But no, she'd rather be volunteering with the goddamn walking dead than sitting with her Dad or even going out for dinner. Who does that? Choose that kinda life. That's the problem, man. She's confused. Just like her mother."

He pulls another Dyson out of the closet and takes it into his bedroom.

"Everyone is just too confused. So, it's not even like it's her fault, you know?" Last Call says. "'She's young, but to just see her rotting away there with them? Well, that's gotta be lonely for her. I worry about that. I think I worry more than I should. Shoulda, coulda, woulda, right?"

I begin climbing into my sleeping bag. Paul turns off another light, starts turning on the vacuum cleaners. I'm too tired to ask him why. I once slept with a girl who had all her stuffed animals face away from the bed when I stayed over, except for the elephants. They watched.

"You alright if I leave these on? That alright?"

He's faltering now. I watch the beers sliding up behind his eyes, little capillaries bursting one by one. I can smell the hops and the gin dripping from his forehead and his pits. Paul's shoulders shudder and wilt as he turns to the bedroom. I just want to sleep, but he isn't finished talking yet. All around me are humming machines trying to tell him to go to goddamn bed.

"I need to go hit the sack now. But like, don't get freaked out by the machines, alright? Hey, you know where the bathroom is and everything? You good with pillows?"

"I'm fine, man," I say and close my eyes again.

"Alright. Hope you feel—well, feels like some kinda home, right?"

Paul turns off another light. He's got a talking fish mounted over the door, but no batteries are left in it. The sale sticker is still attached. I can't find the TV remote under all the sweaters.

"Hey, Paul, man? You there?"

"Yeah?"

"Why not just like leave the TV on, or like a radio, man?" I ask. "You really need all these going? I don't want to ask but like, well, what about your hydro bill?"

I don't have to quite yell over the sound of the vacuums. True to Paul's word, there isn't a Hoover anywhere to be found. Just a steady uninterrupted thrum making the coffee table vibrate under my hand. The sensation travels up my arm and I feel it shake my teeth softly.

"Huh?"

"What about the TV? Why not just leave it on?"

He just stares back at me with his mouth open, tongue poking out the black gap in his teeth. His jaw swings loose back and forth, trying to get a hold on the words.

"TV ain't—don't got—doesn't have any presence man. Just noise. You don't feel nothing from it. Doesn't pull anything at all. I can turn them all down if you want."

"Nah buddy, never mind. Wake me up before you get break-fast, okay? I make good eggs."

"Sure. Scrambled," Last Call says. "You know how to do scram-bled, right?"

He closes the door. The room goes dark. I pull my sleeping bag over my head. The constant hum works its way into my cells like a quiet chain reaction with no end. Somewhere I hear moaning. The hair on my knuckles prickles up and the sound surrounds me as I close my eyes, swaddled in vibrations. Out there in the trembling air, Last Call dreams of voices he will recognize in sunlight, of hearts instead of motors, of daughters and the soothing weight of a hammer in a hand that no longer shakes. The moon outside is hiding from me behind the snow.

I am dreaming of a better place than this.

SIMCOE FURRIERS

OWEN FRELL SPENT HIS DAYS SURROUNDED BY DEATH. THE HIDES of beavers, bears and a lone wolf were stretched out around him. Dust covered most of the lights in the shop on Simcoe. The windows were still covered in soap scum and the open sign was unlit. Occasionally, it would sputter to life, but the tubes were so jammed with dead flies by now, you could barely make out the letters. Sometimes Owen and Jerry would break down the beasts themselves, but usually the furs arrived on their own, still dripping. It was their job to resurrect the fragments.

There was some amateur taxidermist across town who liked to call the two of them butchers and hacks, but he was the one repurposing pets as furniture, so what did he know anyway? Owen liked to tell his wife Connie they were creating art. They were recycling and reusing what Mother Nature gave them, taking the corpses of the dead and bringing back some life for thirty bucks an hour. Just like his father had before him within these very walls.

"Now I don't want a coat or a hat or any of that shit. I just want it made into a rug. Can you handle that, or is Jerry just running his mouth as usual? He said you guys would do it gratis."

The man in front of Frell was short, but his neck was ringed with wasted muscles. Something was inside him, slowly draining all of the colour from his skin. He was like one of those boxers you see on TV twenty years after their last match, a sneer replaced with drool and drooping eyes. This man's eyes weren't blank holes though. His blue pupils combed over everything in the shop, slowly piecing Frell together and pulling him apart. This was a man used to taking an inventory, a man used to disposing of his own waste. The man smacked his hands together and laughed. His hands were filled with fine white scars and misplaced knuckles.

"You can handle this or should I find someone else?"

"It shouldn't be a problem," Frell said. Jerry was still hiding in the bathroom.

Two old bearded bikers had carried the corpse through the back door. They brought the head through last. Tufts from the mane caught on the hinges, but they made it fit. The lion lay on the floor before Frell now, its jaws cracked open and its stomach split by some mechanical force. Ribs and tiny shards of glass poked through the skin. Frell stepped on its tail and waited for the creature to roar. The short man popped pills into his mouth and crunched them twice.

"I wanna keep the head, so you're going to have to put it on ice or something for now. You got a freezer we can use here, or what?"

"Yeah, it has a few beavers in there still, but I think the head will fit."

The short man nodded and pulled his hat off. Small sprigs of red hair dotted his scalp.

"Alright then. You tell Jerry he can come out of the bathroom. We're leaving."

The three men turned and the door slammed shut behind them. Frell sighed and looked down at the body on the floor. The lion's eyes were still intact. Someone had hit it with a car, but the cold and snow had kept it in pretty good condition. The rug would probably cover a king-sized bed when it was finished. The tail was longer than Frell's arm. That would be the first thing to go. The whole thing smelled like diesel fuel and expired beef, but he was used to that by now. His father had come home every day with a new batch of blood and fluid on his hands. It was the dust they used to treat the furs that killed him off, the alum salts and soda ash trapped inside his battered lungs. All the sinks were stained a sickly beige in his parents' house.

"You can come out now Jerry, you don't need to keep hiding. We'll get this sorted out."

From the bathroom, all Frell could hear was Jerry emptying his stomach.

"How do you lose ten thousand playing bingo?"

The lion's corpse had been stripped of its hide. They broke the body down into heavy pieces and stashed them in garbage bags for the incinerator. They shared the facilities with a few other shops in town. Half of them were breaking by-laws, dumping paint and old toxic cleaners down into the flames until green clouds and bursts of sulphur emerged out into the dark. No one was going to question the chunks of flesh. Most would just assume they skinned another bear.

"You bet high. You gotta take advantage during those lightning rounds. I mean, there are rumours some of the balls are weighted so they fall out faster, but you never know which ones they are and this old biddy, Mrs. Castle, well, she plays like sixteen cards at a time, and she says that its always the eights that get weighted. You know, 58, 68, 18. So you look for a card with those and then you commit to it."

Jerry was a kid who stumbled into the shop one day, asking if you could make a hat out of a squirrel. There were always boys like this, ever since Frell's father had opened the store thirty years ago. They all thought they were ready, thought it might make them tough to see how easily the skin can come apart from the flesh, how all the muscles look mechanical once the surface is stripped away. They usually left with their lunch on the floor or their eyes cast down toward their shoes. Some of them even came back as activists, occasionally screaming murderer through the mail slot or egging the windows. They weren't ready for the eyes staring back at them from the table or the smell of the salts and dyes filling up their sinuses. Jerry stuck it out though, searching for dollars and loose change he could take to his mother who spent fifteen hours a day in the bingo hall. Once she passed from some kind of aneurysm that left her face so twisted she had to have a closed casket, Jerry inherited her seat at the head table. All his friends were seniors now, and they all had a plan for him to make the big bucks, the real score. Everybody knew the bingo halls in Larkhill were crooked. You just had to figure out the system.

You just had to put some money on the line.

"And somehow you end up with ten thousand owing?"

"It gets away from you," Jerry said. He held a skinning knife in his hand. Frell's hands had begun to shake lately. Connie noticed it at breakfast one morning. She said it was all those powders they were tossing around in the shop to clean the furs. Frell hadn't said anything. His wife believed it was the shop that had made him so feeble, the shop that was stealing their future even as it preserved everyone else's fucking trophies. Connie liked to call it the trophy shop or the morgue. She didn't drop off his lunch anymore, and there were no notes on the fridge. They were still trying for a kid, but only with all the lights off in the bedroom. Her days at the Henderson law firm downtown were always getting longer, and Frell was used to watching *Jeopardy* by himself now. He always lost it all on the Daily Doubles.

"And this is supposed to repay the favour?" Frell said. He watched as Jerry stretched the fur out over the custom rack they'd had to build out of spare pieces. The lion's hide was holding up nicely, but it was going to be a bitch to pick out all the glass from its belly. Frell ran a hand through the fur and pinched a sharp shiny piece between his thick fingers.

"Well, some of it, you know. I still got some other stuff to deal with…"

Frell nodded. Jerry always owed someone. This job was going to come out of his pay.

"But nothing with the little man?"

"Who? Crane? No, he's just the one everything goes through. And he's not that little. You've seen his hands right? That's not from fighting, that's just some weird sickness he's got in him. I ain't worried 'bout him. It's more the two big tunas with him. They got a toolbox for all kinds of… well, they don't use it for dishwasher repair, you know?"

Frell turned and pulled on his coat. He was tired of the shop. The flies in the open sign had somehow multiplied since the short man had come by for his visit. The street was usually abandoned except for a comic shop on the corner and the endless line of garbage trucks that passed by on their way to the dump. Their smell wasn't too different from the animals. The short man had been the only customer all week and Frell wasn't even getting paid.

"Remember, Jerry, you owe me on this one."

The soaped glass door slammed shut before Jerry could respond.

Owen Frell let the messages play while he tried to make a sandwich. The ham in the fridge was still good, but he didn't trust the old cheddar Connie had forgotten on the counter. One of the calls was from some old timer expressing his condolences for Frell's old man. He was still out in Winnipeg when they had the funeral, but he'd heard it was the heart. He heard the old man went out in his sleep or something. Frell knew that much was true, but he also knew his father wasn't too peaceful near the end. Something was in his brain, something that left him chewing on pillows and asking about all the creatures he'd skinned and remade. He wanted to know if they were happy. Frell deleted the message and chose the honey mustard.

Jeopardy was muted in the living room. There were no pickles for the sandwich and the next message was about Connie's credit cards. Frell had cut most of them up, but he was sure she still had one or two kicking around. He had stopped caring. If she wanted to spend it on fancy lunches or those dresses from designers he couldn't name, that was all right with him. She said she wanted to live and if that meant cocktails after work and three-course dinners, so be it. He just wanted to have his fridge stocked. The clock said it was 7:30, but he didn't expect her to come home any time soon. They still tried once or twice a week, but it usually didn't last too long. The sounds they made barely rattled the headboard. No neighbours complained anymore. Frell was getting used to sleeping in his chair. The world didn't seem as overwhelming if he woke up already seated. All he had to do was place his feet firmly on the floor to remind him it was there.

Frell got up to delete the message, but another one began to play before he made it to the old machine. Dr. Iverston's office was just calling to let Connie Frell-Duncan know her results were ready. They provided a phone number, but there was no address. Frell pressed the button to save the message, but his hands shook a little. His lungs rattled and he tried not to hack phlegm up all over the house phone. Frell still refused to get a cell phone. He refused call waiting and he refused all attempts to address him by mail. He didn't want the world to find him here.

Alex Trebek was still explaining a Daily Double question to his contestants when Frell returned to sit in the dark living room. His hands still smelled like blood, even after washing them twice at the kitchen sink. One of the players decided to bet all he could on the question, but Frell still had the TV on mute. It was something about the space race. He couldn't read the text. Frell stretched out his legs and placed his wide feet on the coffee table. He knew Dr. Iverston was not their family doctor. Frell had never heard of him. The man on the television knew the answer. Frell could see it in his eyes. He imagined it was something about Russians and a dog spat out into the darkness of space. Frell though it should have been a lion. Maybe someone would have heard it out there in the dark. Someone would have saved it from the cold instead of leaving it to die all by itself. The contestant smiled and Frell knew the game was settled.

Trebek could only shake his head. Wrong.

Frell tried to take another bite of his sandwich, but he couldn't control his hands. He watched it bounce off his chest and land on the floor. The mustard would stain the rug. Connie would leave him. The doctor's secretary had basically said as much. Frell considered getting up and pulling the sandwich off the floor. He considered driving down to Connie's office and asking her about that doctor and those late nights and why she'd cried so hard at his father's funeral if it was all just for laughs anyway. He considered praying to God for a son or something he could call a legacy—something permanent. Owen Frell considered all things, but instead, turned off the television. The minutes passed and he waited for the door to open. He waited until his eyes closed and in the darkness, he dreamed about a toolbox filled with all his friends and family, each one skinned alive and bleeding slowly. He asked them why nobody warned him about this. He posed the question, but all he got were groans in response. He wanted an answer.

The toolbox closed and swallowed him whole.

They never bothered with security at the shop. The broken windows were a new addition. Someone had painted MURDERERS in red across the glass door. All the hides were covered in bright red splotches. It was dawn. All the broken glass glowed pink. Three beavers and a wolf hide were ruined by broad splashes of paint. The clients would moan, but they would understand. There were always a few kids in town who decided animals didn't deserve to have their hides ripped off by old men like Owen Frell. They thought those animals could feel and think and believe in all kinds of things like a good diet and proper grooming procedures. They believed in the circle of life and all that good organic shit you had to pay double for at the grocery store. And there were mornings where Frell wanted to agree with those kids, mornings filled with stacks of foxes and the smell of their intestines still full of mice and chicks and baby rabbits.

This wasn't one of those mornings.

"Oh shit, oh shit, you gotta be kidding me," Jerry moaned. He stalked in circles around the ruined hide of the lion. His eyes were red like he'd been smoking, but it was just tears and a bit of rage pouring down his cheeks. Frell spat on the floor. He still had insurance. This wasn't the end of the world. If the world was going to end, it would have done so last night. It would have exploded from the very centre of his living room and obliterated every living thing in sight.

But he was still here. And so was Jerry.

"You'll make it up to him in another way, Jerry," Frell said. "It's just bingo anyway, it's not the worst thing in the world. I'm sure he'll forgive you for this one. We will find another—"

"Another fucking what, Owen? A fucking lion? Are you kidding me? This was my one goddamn chance and then some little shit… you shoulda seen this coming!"

Jerry was dancing around in a circle like he had to piss. His feet bounced up and down. He held a piece of the stretching frame in his hand like a cross.

"I shoulda seen… excuse me?"

"Never fucking mind, alright? You don't ever listen, do you? I told you we shoulda… Look, Crane isn't going to forgive anything, alright? He doesn't do that. It isn't part of his game. This was like my… fucking Monopoly 'get out of jail free' card, alright? Like a one-time pass."

Frell shook his head and sat down on a stool. The paint made everything look new.

"I can't stay here, Owen. He's going to come here and he's going to see this shit…"

"And what?" Frell said. He was still surveying the damage. At least they hadn't attacked the electrical or the water main. He coughed twice before he saw the heavy wood swinging toward his face. Jerry was weeping now, but he didn't stop swinging until Frell was laid out on the floor.

Frell could hear Jerry fumbling around his body, searching for the keys. The pain was in his head, but it was more like a tide than a wave. It was pulling him back and forth, clutching his tongue so he couldn't speak. Frell wanted to tell the kid about his own father and how the man had tried to outrun a life of dealing in hides and roadkill. He had tried all those medicines you see at 4:00 AM on the Shopping Network and stuff some old psychic downtown had offered him for fifty bucks a gram. He had gone through the last three years of his life running from whatever was slowing his heart, whatever dust had gathered around his lungs and his arteries, clutching at them like manacles. Physiotherapy, acupuncture—all of those treatments were just distractions. None of them slowed the world down.

Frell heard Jerry pulling at the office door. He heard him cursing Frell, the bingo hall and that godforsaken lion. He heard the safe crack open and all Frell wanted to tell Jerry was that you cannot run forever. You cannot keep up that pace.

On his way out the door, Jerry paused for a second over Frell's body. Frell tried to stretch out his lips to form a word before Jerry's boot connected with his head. Frell's body slumped back down amongst the spoiled hides. In the fading darkness, he did not hear Jerry drive away.

Owen Frell pulled the lion's head out of the freezer. Its blank eyes didn't judge him. He ran his hands along its sharp teeth, feeling the cool touch of the gums against his fingers. Some of the back teeth were beginning to go black. The tongue was rough against his thumb. The short man would be back soon for his lion. He would find the hide torn and ripped and stained with bright red paint, tiny flaps of skin scattered around the shop. Jerry was gone by now, his notes and all the cash from the safe tucked under the seat of his mother's Monte Carlo, headed towards Atlantic City or some backwoods town where no one had ever heard of high stakes bingo. Connie wasn't answering her phone and the thing in her belly, or whatever it was, wasn't going to call him Dad.

Owen Frell carried the lion's head over to his work table, still splattered with bright red house paint. The lion wasn't here to judge him. It didn't ask him to stop by the store for more milk, or to make an appointment with the fertility doctor. It didn't ask him if furriers were trapped in a dying trade, if they were soon to join the cobblers and the butchers and the knife sharpeners and all those fishermen out in Newfoundland on the unemployment line. The lion just gazed out from frozen eyes and accepted everything as it was, everything as it would be.

Owen Frell placed his head inside the lion's massive jaws. He laid his unshaven cheek against its sandy tongue and listened to the echo of his breathing. Eventually, the short man would arrive with a toolbox and some pliers. He would want to know where Jerry went and about what had happened to his rug. Owen Frell didn't know how to answer those kinds of questions. He just wanted to rest. The lion's mouth was cool and quiet. The short man could bring his tools and his giants and all their heavy hammers to break the tiny bones inside Frell's feet—it didn't really matter now. There was no one left to carry on his name, to strip the foxes and raccoons brought in by farmers and teenagers with too much time on their hands. There was no one left to make something out of all these mutilated bodies, to reclaim them from roadkill incinerators and hackneyed taxidermists. All those glowing coats would go to waste. Frell sighed and felt the powder rattle around inside his lungs. His father said it wasn't the lungs that took you though— it was the heart. It slowed you down. Made you shake worse than DTs toward the end. All the damage centred there eventually, a whole life coalescing inside hardened arteries. Frell wrapped his arms around the lion's head and closed his eyes. He waited.

The lion refused to bite.

THE WEEK FOOTBALL STOPPED

DAD SAT IN THE GREEN LAWN CHAIR AND TOLD ME I WASN'T MARCHING right. I wasn't lifting my knees high enough. The gravel driveway was the perfect place to practice these drills. Mom had taken the car back in July and the driveway hadn't been used much since.

That was the week football stopped. A week after dust swallowed a city whole somewhere across the country while we tried to watch highlights on a Tuesday night. I didn't mind missing the games too much. Our satellite dish was dead. It hung from the roof like a broken hearing aid amongst the old Christmas lights. Some nights I plugged them in to look at the yellows and pinks—former greens and reds that had expired. Raccoons liked to play in the Christmas lights. They gnawed at the cables.

We lived down by the airport. Mom said we'd never sell the house with all that goddamn noise. Dad said he liked the sound—a constant hum like a pulse. But there were no planes flying that week either.

After three hours in the driveway, Dad went inside to wait for a phone call. They would need him after this, he said.

"Football isn't coming back, Frankie. Not after this. Not after what happened."

Instead we watched taped games. We watched highlight reels and speeches from the greats. Most of all we watched Jim Brown.

We watched the rushes over and over as Brown dodged every tackle or pushed for that extra yard with three defensive linemen clinging to his back. Dad said the closest most men could get to any true conflict was in a football game. That football players were the closest anyone could get to battle without any real blood. And nobody wanted to see that blood, he said. They just wanted everything up to that point—everything but the aftermath.

"And you know what, Frankie?"

He got up from his chair, swinging his bad leg forward. Its metal joints squeaked.

"You watch a game now and everyone is running out of bounds or taking a knee. No one wants to get hit anymore. Not ever."

His breath smelled like TV dinners and mouthwash.

"Nobody knows how to take a hit like Jim Brown."

He started walking me to school the week football stopped. I was only ten. He wore his helmet and his desert uniform. Prepared at all times. We had to leave an hour early to make it there on time. He worried about missing any important calls, but he trusted the answering machine. He knew they would need his help like before. The sky still was empty and you could hear the bugs if you were up in the middle of the night. No planes.

"They'll know where to find me when they need me. They'll come."

I avoided his eyes as we walked.

"Who played in the Pro Bowl every single season he played in the NFL?"

"Jim Brown."

"Who was the first player to ever break the 10,000 mark for rushing yards?"

"Jim Brown."

He made me wear a football helmet. Just like Jim Brown, I would always be prepared for that blindside tackle. It was orange and too big for my skull. It made me into a walking target.

Each day I waited for the kids at school to call him names— names like the ones Mom yelled at him over the phone, the ones that made him snap records in half and tear up the carpeting at home. But they never did. They just stared until one of the big ones asked him if he could call him RoboCop.

Dad stood above them, his metal ankle showing beneath the pants he'd pulled up a little too high. He'd said the older you got the higher the pants were supposed to go. He thought that was funny.

"Is he a bad guy?" Dad asked.

"No, no he's like the ultimate good guy—sort of. They have to rebuild him after he's murdered and then he comes back and he—"

"So he's not a bad guy?"

"No. Definitely not."

When he walked me home after school that day, Dad told me he had rented all the *RoboCop* movies. The best one, he said, was the first because RoboCop could never really die. And so RoboCop became another staple of our daily training. Dad left it on repeat inside the house. I marched up and down the driveway listening to the dialogue in between his commands.

"Dead or alive, you're coming with me."

Football came back though. Other kids at school told me the stats. They spouted off numbers and names to one another and I just sat there unable to keep up. They showed me newspaper pictures and magazines full of tackles. Dad did not believe me though. He said that they were lying. It was all part of another scam, another way to rip off the fans. It was just a mirage, a mess they broadcast to keep anyone from asking any questions.

When I woke up one morning, the television was broken. The power cord was torn in half. The newspaper had been torn into little wisps of paper that floated around under the ceiling fan. There were bandages stuck in the kitchen sink, as if someone had tried to push them down the drain. Dad lay on the floor sleeping with his leg in his arms. I went to school without him and I didn't wear the helmet.

Dad stopped walking me to school after that. He said he couldn't take people lying to his face every day. The newspapers piled up on the porch and so he burned them in the fire pit behind the house. I started taking off the helmet as soon as I was out of sight. No one thought it was funny anymore. Kids began to throw dirt clods at my head. Dad was no longer RoboCop. He stayed at home with a dirty hand cradling the telephone and his metal leg lying beside him on the floor. He waited for a call from the government and befriended telemarketers.

Dad caught me without the helmet one afternoon. He could see me from the roof as I made my way down the driveway.

"Put that back on, Frankie!"

"No, it's too hot."

"Put it on!"

"Get off the roof!"

"I'll get off the roof when you put that goddamn helmet back on, do you hear me? Don't make me come down there and get you to do it, Frankie!"

"Why are you on the roof?"

It must have taken him an hour to climb the ladder without falling. His army helmet was tilted to the side on his head. His fatigues matched the trees that swayed around him with the heavy wind.

"Who said you could ask questions?"

He was fiddling with the satellite.

"Okay, I'll put the helmet back on, Dad. Come down, please."

"I am not coming down 'til I fix this."

"Fix what?"

He stumped across the shingles, clutching the useless chimney for support.

"How was I supposed to know they don't use phones anymore? Now it's all satellites."

He had a toolbox up there with him.

"No, they aren't going to call. You need to get down from there."

He grunted and stared back at me.

"Is it because of this, huh?"

He yanked up his pant leg.

"No, no…"

"I gave them this Frankie, and now they don't want me back? Is that what you are saying? You're the messenger now delivering their divine goddamn wisdom?"

"No I'm not the messenger. I'm not, I'm not anything. I'm just…"

"Yeah, you're nothing. But I'm not nothing, Frankie, even like this. You think this holds me back? It doesn't Frankie, it fucking doesn't. I don't care what your mother says. It won't stop me from getting what's mine. I'm not nothing, Frankie, alright?"

I noticed I was standing on the oil patch Mom had left behind.

"Dad, they brought football back. It all came back."

"That doesn't mean anything! That means nothing! They are all cowards now, running off the sidelines because no one wants to drive for that extra frikkin' yard. They're all so afraid of getting hurt that they don't even know how to play anymore. Look at all the timeouts they're calling! It's just a load of bullshit now, Frankie! Don't you see it? It's not football. It's nothing!"

"Come down! Alright? I get it. I get it!"

"They are going to call me!"

"No, they aren't. They aren't going to call you. Not through the satellite!"

"Do you see any planes up there Frankie? How come they haven't been flying? How come the television isn't working anymore? How come they have buildings falling apart out there? Everything is on fire there. Everything is on fire and covered in ash. They call it dust, but it's ash from everything they've burned. And you're telling me they don't need me because of this? I gave them this. They have to take me. They have to."

In the distance, I heard a rumble. The trees began to shake.

"Dad, they aren't trying to call you through the satellite. They aren't trying to call you through the phone either. Nobody is calling you except Mom."

"How do you know? You're at school all day!"

The sound began to drown him out. A plane cracked through the sky overhead and I watched him lose his balance. His bad leg shifted underneath him as the shingles rattled. He fell backwards. I never heard the scream. My ears were filled with roaring engines.

I ran inside to dial the phone, but it was already ringing. I picked up.

"Hey, honey, just calling to check in on you two. The car ran out of gas again. We're in Texas. I was hoping your Dad could wire us some money or—"

I hung up the phone and sat down on the floor. Dad was laid out flat in the backyard. His good leg was broken in three places. He was screaming about the planes and the dust. I tried to block out the sound. I remembered Mom taking the car and telling me to come with her. Didn't matter how big her heart was, she'd said, this place was toxic. I remembered finding bloody gauze in the toilet and a dead raccoon tied up in the old Christmas lights after she left. Its legs were broken. Something had been eating it in the middle of the night. And I saw my father lying out there in the sun now, his good leg bleeding and his eyes full of nothing but me and Jim Brown and some pain he couldn't explain, couldn't parse into words outside of the broken dialects he'd chosen. No one was calling him and he was mangled. He'd always been mangled. His metal leg had bounced down into the ravine somewhere, and soon the sun was going to go down. Planes were flying again, worlds were moving again, cities were falling into dust all over again—new cities I couldn't name. Everything stayed the same even as it changed.

Dad was still quoting RoboCop when they put him on the stretcher.

"They'll fix you. They fix everything," he said.

I didn't tell him any different.

SATIN LIVES!

A RABBIT LOOKS A LOT SMALLER WITHOUT ITS HEAD.

"We already took him downtown. If you wanna bail him out tonight…"

It's all in the ears. Without those, you could mistake the corpse for a woodchuck or an overfed squirrel. You might even think it was a rat if it wasn't for the tail.

You might not even see it in the dark.

The rabbit's throat is cut ragged though. Bits of fur are scattered around a loose pentagram of gravel in the elementary school parking lot. Some of the stones look wet.

"You know if it happens again, they aren't going to keep looking the other way."

This is the third rabbit in as many months. I don't know what he does with the heads. The local cops have come to recognize the signature. We used to go to school here, back before Dad decided he was going to go work in some oil fields. Peter has painted the bricks with the rabbit's blood. One of the officers is trying to wash away the ragged letters. The blood runs down through the shoddy brickwork. I pick up a few stones off the ground. They are cold.

"I know," I say to the sergeant, the same one who calls me when Peter has broken into the hospital cafeteria or stolen all the red chillies from the Korean grocery again. The sergeant always sighs before identifying himself over the phone. "I will talk to him about it."

"You're going to have to do more than talk," the sergeant says. "You're going have to commit him or get him some help. I can't keep writing mischief when this shit goes down."

The red letters are five feet high. The lines fade toward the end of the phrase. A rabbit only has so much blood to give. I don't know where he finds them in this city.

"My sister, she's got a kid like that, you know? That's why I wanted to give him a break. Some people just ain't right. Not their fault. Could be something in their... uhm, DNA? You wanna call it that? Some people are just born a few pieces short of the full set, you know?"

The wall reads *SATIN LIVES!* in sloppy block letters. The exclamation mark is dotted with something like a skull. My brother still can't spell.

"I know what you mean," I say, and kick at the pentagram until it becomes a star.

When I was ten, Peter slammed my hand in the bathroom door. I think the first time it was an accident. I like to tell myself that. The next five rapid slams crushed three of my right fingers. The bones pushed through the skin. The world went red and white and he was laughing. Mom said he didn't understand. Peter was always trying so hard to please everyone. He thought it was a good joke. He was only five. I still have my pinkie and the thumb.

After the first surgery, my Mom told me, "Everything heals given time." When she left to go ask the doctor about my medication, Peter came over to inspect my hand. He asked me where the middle fingers were hiding. I told him they'd been swallowed up by the doctor. That they were a sacrifice to some frightening God, the same one we read about in church before Mom stopped going to Mass. Peter always liked to listen to me talk. Lying in that hospital bed, staring at what was once a hand, I told him the real reason Dad had left: he wasn't really Peter's father. Peter had black hair, didn't he? He had blue eyes too, right? Dad was blond. His eyes were green.

Peter nodded. I was lying there trying to erase stories I'd heard about oil fields or Africa or the unexplored rivers of the Amazon, whatever Mom decided to tell me that week. I erased a man who liked to read me stories about monsters, about things hiding in the dark, things waiting for you to get lost in the woods or down a sewer drain. Things made of shadows and hate. He read me things about two-faced men and ancient gods bent on destruction, and then he said goodbye. We moved into an apartment after that, one with heavy bathroom doors and only one window.

With sunlight filling the hospital room, I told Peter all about the demon that snuck into our house one night before he was born. The one who looked like a man, the one who made our father flee into the country or into a bottle or wherever he ended up, trussed and beaten and drowned in the Mississippi after a bet went badly. These are the things I liked to imagine.

I told Peter about the seed this man planted in our mother. I told him how it grew and grew until Peter came out screaming, covered in blood. Peter didn't ask me any questions. His eyes didn't grow wide and he didn't turn away. He just nodded. I told him he was born from some beast, some creature bent on corrupting the earth. Did Peter remember church? Did he remember the speech about the mustard seeds and the weeds? Well, someone has to plant those weeds too, Peter. Someone has to spread them across the soil. Peter nodded again. You weren't born the same way I was, I said. That's why you like to kill the flies. That's why you did this to my hand.

"So, we'll hand him over to you for five hundred. Do you have that much on you?" the man behind the desk says. He doesn't look me in the eye. He tries to avoid staring at my right hand.

I keep the money in a jar over the stove. Dina and I have gotten used to this ritual. The money usually gets returned eventually. Folding cardboard boxes all day isn't exactly a career, but it's full time. I work the night shift so I can keep an eye on Peter during the day. She's still working at the pharmacy and tries to stay awake until I get home. Once Mom gave up the ghost, it fell on us to take Peter under our roof.

Houses are cheap down by the highway, and you get used to the constant thrum of traffic running up and down your spine—some new-age, droning lullaby. Sometimes it drowns out Peter's noises, the chanting or scribbling or whatever he is doing in the dark. He doesn't really sleep. He tells me he doesn't like to close his eyes.

"You just can't stay inside, can you buddy?" I say as we climb into the car.

"There's too much out there to see, Al," Peter says. His voice is still high-pitched. He sounds fourteen, but his face is pocked and pitted. "Too many things going wrong. Too many people thinking they understand how the world works. They don't know it's broken."

My brother believed me about the demon thing. He swallowed the entire story and spat it up in classrooms, onto teachers' faces, students' laps and the principal's brand-new Cadillac. He scrawled it on the pews in churches and in the middle of the street with spray paint and claw hammers. Fellow residents in the apartment building began to take the stairs when he got in the elevator. Mom got used to switching schools, driving him to doctors and psychiatrists with lots of diplomas and no explanations. Peter just told them he was born this way. He was born under a sign. He was born a weed. I looked at my hand and didn't say a thing. The doctors never showed me how to use it, so I had to adapt on my own, growing stronger. Peter liked to watch it twitch, watch the tendons slowly return to life. He tried to hold it at night. He learned to whisper my mother's mantra in the dark: everything heals given time.

The streets outside are wet. The blood on the school is still there though. The roads on this side of town all wind into each other, smashing stacks of row houses and tenements together. The medical clinic on the hill overlooks everything below it, surrounded by the last few apartment buildings they've delayed destroying until the weather improves. Those towers are empty now except for the rats and asbestos, waiting to sift its way into our lungs once they bring the stacked concrete down into organized piles. Peter keeps running his fingers over the inside of the window, playing with the condensation, drawing eyes over and over until the glass is full of accusations. I take a corner and avoid what looks like someone's cat split in two across the dividing line. Its eyes don't glow.

"You didn't do that one, did you Pete?"

"Cats are my friends," Peter says, wiping away all the eyes from the glass. "You know that."

We pass a patch of burnt ground in between some old row houses. They are now abandoned due to smoke and water damage. The police spent three weeks harassing us about Peter, insisting he must have got out one night to start the flames. There was gasoline all over the place when the fire crews arrived. Three women and two children died from smoke inhalation. The bodies were found stacked in a pile, according to the officer who knocked at our door. Someone had planned it out in advance. Stacked like kindling were the words he used. I told them Peter didn't do it. He never played with fire much. We kept him locked up pretty well at home. It's mainly boy scouts who learn how to play with the flame, I told the officer. They teach those kids how to burn things down and then give them a badge for it. They even let them practice it for kicks in the woods.

"I just need to collect more seeds," Peter says. "I want to start my own garden."

I ignore his words and continue to drive along the jagged pavement. Mom's grave had to be moved when they expanded the highway out here. It bypasses most of the downtown now, avoiding the coffee shops and strip joints that have congealed between empty tenements and old auto shops. They built these great big green sound barriers to keep out the noise, but those walls just toss the sound further off into nicer neighbourhoods. It's quieter to live close to the six lanes drilled through the core of this place—an old wound reopened for a vivisection. I learn a lot of these words from Peter. His medical textbooks are filled with check marks and ancient runes. I don't know where he finds them all, but he is still learning to read. We don't ask a lot from him.

Our house doesn't have any neighbours—just two plywood husks leering out into the dark. You can find us on a dead end street that backs right up onto the highway's walls. A couple people live at the head of the street, but they gave up talking to us after their dogs started to disappear. Peter tries to be friendly, but Mom never let him out much after a generous guidance counsellor lost an ear during talk therapy. Maybe the judge took pity on him. The deal got knocked down to house arrest. Until Mom passed away, we never saw Peter outside. His only access to the world came from the sound of Mom's television through the walls.

I imagine it was a world of weeds in his mind. The nightly news informed him of broken bodies and sixteen car pileups somewhere down south. It highlighted epidemics sweeping foreign nations and exposed the dangerous spread of flesh-eating disease in tropical climates. People were losing limbs, eyes and their entire facial structure. The sounds gave a voice and a shape to the evils he could not see. It wormed its way through the walls and Mom's attempt at soundproofing. When I picked up Peter two years ago, the entire bedroom was covered in rows and rows of egg cartons. He had dressed each one up in bright red paint. I knew it was paint because blood turns brown after a while. He was drawing images of his father. That's what he told me before the landlord arrived and started talking about a lawsuit.

"Get out, Pete. You cannot be pulling this shit anymore, alright? What would Mom say if she were here, huh? She would not be impressed."

"Where did they put her? When can we go see her?"

Peter liked to visit her grave before the highway uprooted all the corpses in the south end of town. I would watch him for hours in the graveyard while he sat with the tombstone, running his fingers over the inscription—*all things go*. I imagined Peter asking her who his real father was, asking if what I had said was true. Asking about whatever creature had crept into her bed, asking for her to absolve him once again. She was always willing to forgive him. Each wound he left behind, she said she would wait for it to heal. Lawyers were paid off and bondsmen became close allies. Sometimes they slept over after Peter was released. Mom told me he just needed time. He needed to figure out who he was. The world was so busy telling us what we were meant to do, meant to buy, meant to be—Peter had to listen to some voice inside. I showed her what was left of my hand. I asked her to count my fingers.

"I don't know, buddy. They took all the coffins up north. They've still got to sort them out. And the tombstones, too. Gotta make sure everything matches up."

Peter strides ahead of me toward the front door. It's got three locks and a peephole, but we don't get many visitors. I've given up on ordering pizzas.

"They won't do it right, you know. They don't know anything about the dead."

Dina sits at the kitchen table inside. She's got three plastic bags laid out in front of her.

"I discovered where he's been keeping them, Al. With the food. In the freezer. It has to stop. Now. I can't keep finding this shit around the house. What kind of house is it when you can't even have anyone over? Imagine someone from the pharmacy finding this shit in our freezer?"

There are three frozen rabbit heads on the kitchen table. Each one is wrapped up tightly in a plastic bag with elastic. All their eyes are covered in frost. The ears have been pushed down and around their faces like cowls. Peter tries to snatch them off the table, but I knock all three onto the floor. Dina doesn't say anything else. She just looks at her hands and shakes her head.

"What did we talk about, Peter?"

He won't look me in the eye. The kitchen light is buzzing above us. The three heads are glowing on the floor. He wants to scoop them up, but I press him back up against the green refrigerator. He starts to whimper a little. Each time he breaks one of the rules, we have to enforce a punishment. Six beady eyes watch as I drag him out of the kitchen by his hair.

"Put them down the disposal, Dina. I don't want anyone finding them in the garbage. I don't think we'll be able to explain it. Not after he brought all those cats inside last time."

I've had to explain a lot to Dina. Our first date involved a visit to the city jail when Mom couldn't get off her shift to pick my brother up. At first she thought it was kind of cool. Peter was like a shaman, she said. Dina told me about black magic in her basement with friends from high school, about an aunt whose psychic readings were so accurate the woman was run out of her village back in Albania. Dina wanted to believe Peter knew what he was doing. She wanted to believe in a world where his chaos had a pattern. Time destroys all patterns though—eventually all you see is one unending line. Occasionally, I get phone calls on my break. Dina finds birds stuffed inside our oven, or Bible pages plastered to the bathroom walls.

She's given up on patterns and shamans. She just wants to get the stains out fast.

"I need them!" Peter screams. I drag him with my good hand toward the old den at the back of this failing house. We spent three weeks reinforcing its walls with two-by-fours and old deck furniture before Peter moved in. The ceiling is covered with soundproofing and insulation. Peter has pissed in every corner, so we bleach it once a week. The chemical scent rushes out in a cloud as I open the door. There is a mattress on the floor with a plastic bucket lying beside it. Peter is pleading with me now. His hands are groping at my waist, but we don't feed him much these days. His muscles are shrivelled. You can see them through the skin.

The door is heavy. I invested in a fire door after he broke the first one down. Sometimes the lock slips and he sneaks out, but usually we maintain a vigil. Dina talks about surveillance footage, but I don't want any evidence of this. I don't want anything to remain.

"Give them back, let me take them. I need to plant them!"

I slam the door, twisting the lock with what's left of my right hand. Peter is screaming again.

"I need them! I need them!"

I know it's just a matter of waiting. Dina and I are expecting our first yowling ball of flesh this summer. The doctor says it's going to be a boy. She wants to name him Aldous. I don't ask her why. I want to name him Peter. Maybe give that name a second chance.

"They are mine! Someone needs to plant the weeds!"

I can hear my brother's fists banging on the walls. I try to ignore the sound and turn on the TV. I watch the nightly news as they survey the bloody markings my brother left behind. The reporters have begun to call him the Great Satin. One newscaster giggles at the name. The camera zooms in close on the letters, but it avoids the headless rabbit corpse. I close my eyes and flex the remains of my right hand. Sometimes I can pretend the fingers are still there.

"Let me out, you stupid fuck! I need them!" my brother screams from behind our homemade padded walls. The lady on the TV talks about the recent graveyard transplant. A few corpses have gone missing, but authorities assure the community all the bodies will be recovered in due time. Dina is trying to sleep in the bedroom wearing industrial ear protection. Her door is leaning open. The headset looks like someone melted orange rabbit ears onto her skull. She says she wants to move, says she wants to leave this place. I've told her all of this is temporary.

"I need them!"

Given time, everything dies.

KINGSTON ROAD

A WEED WHACKER WAKES ME UP AT FOUR AM AND I KNOW IT'S Harley again. He's trying to get the Bulgarian family out of Unit 16; they have been sleeping with earplugs for the past two weeks of this ongoing siege. Harley doesn't wanna call the cops because he still has a few plants growing in the ceiling of Unit 5. Last week he told me that he could taste the buds whenever he pushed his head up into the panels. The moisture makes the ceiling tiles sag over my bed.

I roll over and try to cover my ears with a pillow. The Woodson stands in a long row of motels down Kingston Road, boxed in by the One-Nite Inn and the Cardinal House. In the former outskirts of the city, now overgrown with townhouses and gas stations, these little shacks pay down the mortgage by renting out rooms equipped with hotplates and beer fridges, stuffing Eastern European families into twin bed suites with no hot water and calling them homes. My neighbours routinely bash their bodies against the wall while their three kids pretend to sleep in the same room. A couple days ago we were all trapped in the elevator again, but I didn't bother to bring it up. Everything smelled like meat and chlorine. A man with a moustache kept slamming his fat hand against all the buttons every time the elevator rattled. Two tiny kids stared at their feet and poked each other. The Woodson only has two floors, but the stairs are filled with broken furniture and car parts Harley hasn't figured out how to sell. I always take the elevator.

Chlorine filters through the entire place. Harley says the pool keeps everyone happy. He skims forgotten underwear, plastic bags and loose Kleenexes out of the water every morning. I search the bottom for change each night before I go to bed and try to figure out who goes swimming with coins inside their pockets.

The weed whacker hits the side of the building and shrieks out some displeasure. Raccoons respond from the roof next door. The Bulgarians remain fast asleep. They refuse to pay for the fish stolen from the aquarium in the lobby. Harley says he has it on video and suspects the oldest one sold it to another family in the One-Nite next door. Harley could smell it frying.

I open my window and look down into the courtyard. Harley's got orange headphones over his ears, the kind I used to wear on the farm when we fired up the combine. I try yelling to him, but he keeps restarting the weed whacker again and again. He pokes the whirring wire end against the building again to make it scream so I slam the window shut.

Outside in the hall, the air-conditioner and ice machine compete with one another to shake the wallpaper loose once and for all. Every six minutes, the ice machine's compressor kicks over like a police boot punching through the door. Harley tells all the tenants they'll get used to the sound. He calls it ambience. He said the same thing about the fish.

I walk down the hall toward the elevator; the hallway is free from the mechanical torture going on outside. The T-shirt I've got on says Reddon Raiders. It's long enough to cover the holes in my boxers, but it still smells like manure and guilt and all the other stuff you find back home. Reddon is miles away from Kingston Road; no one asks about that place. Bulgarians don't inquire about family history or question young men they just met about the girls they used to take back into the fields. I don't have a phone. Don't have any calls about hospital bills or visitation rights or all the tests they want me to take for proof of whatever.

I pay for my room on a weekly basis and let Harley tell me all about his uncle who owned the place. Apparently, this uncle used to do a lot of laps in the pool and died at forty-seven in the middle of a backstroke. He fixed Chevys and worked with some Armenians to skim the local bingo hall. Harley was the one who found him floating in the shallows. Harley says it was the best thing that ever happened to him and I believe it. He spent most of the inheritance on hydroponic lamps and a tattoo of his dead dog Chuckles.

There is a baby in the hallway.

It stands right in front of me and doesn't blink. The ice machine kicks over again, but the baby doesn't move. It cocks its head and follows me as I back slowly towards my door. Things like this aren't supposed to follow you. The baby only wears a diaper. It teeters back and forth; tiny feet sink deep into the shaggy orange carpeting.

"Uhm, hey buddy, err... Baby? Where's your Mom?"

The baby takes a few more steps toward me and then falls directly onto its face.

"Shit, shit, shit... Okay, you okay?"

I lift the sweaty little bundle off of the floor. Its sticky face is covered with carpet lint. Drool drips onto my shoulder. The baby sags between my hands like a sack of dead leaves.

"Can you tell me what room you came from? Tell me something."

The baby only groans and clucks into my ear.

I consider banging on doors, calling out names, all the good things I should do and then I remember the fat man in the elevator and the smell of his skin. The kids refused to look me in the eye as we sat there for an hour waiting for Harley to pry the door open. Sometimes you hear things in the dark. Harsh and splintered things in the wet air that float through the Woodson.

I avoid the elevator and take the stairs two at a time, dodging the broken chairs and discarded *Penthouse* issues stacked up on the landing. The baby babbles over my shoulder, but the words are just syllables strung together; they don't display a pattern. The baby is wet and I can feel something leaking onto my skin. It's deadweight against my chest. A bit of fur rustles in a pile of paper under the last set of stairs, but I ignore it and step out into the lobby. Moist air coats my face and the empty aquarium belches hot bubbles toward the ceiling. The NO VACANCY sign hisses every time a fruit fly ventures close to its neon heat.

Inside the manager's office, the clock reads 4:15 AM and there are pictures of Harley with various tattoo models. He has printed his face onto the images with women straddling his chest and pressing inked fingers against their pursed and puckered lips. Harley's face is the same in every picture. Some of the women have been cut into jagged pieces and line the edges of the frames. Harley is smiling.

I sit the baby down on a beanbag chair in the corner. Piss soaks my shirt, but the baby still refuses to cry. Its eyes follow the lava lamp in the corner as the red goo combines and separates over and over again. I search for the phone and try to avoid all the nachos littering Harley's desk.

"Yo, what are you doing in the office, man? What's with the fuckin' baby? You know the Eurotrash still won't give up, eh? I even tried tossing rocks at the windows, but they are holed up in there good and tight. I'm thinking of breaking down the door tomorrow—middle of the night covert ops shit. Maybe a baseball bat or something. Who are they gonna go to anyway, right? Illegal shits got no choice. I'll ask Lazlo about it tomorrow when he has new tenants for me."

Harley has the orange headphones tucked around his neck. The weed whacker dangles from his left hand. The baby continues watching the lava lamp in the corner.

"Just looking for the phone, man. Found this frickin' baby upstairs just all by itself. Just standing there. Freaking crazy, man. Just standing there. You got a cell or something?"

Back in Reddon, we had a calf get out one night. Somehow it slipped through the gate and headed toward the iced-over pond all the cattle drank from in the summer. Nobody heard anything at the time. We found the hole in the morning; a jagged gash splintered in every direction by the animal's weight. It went down deep. I didn't bother looking for a bottom.

"You want the phone? You calling for what? I don't want any cops in here, man. You know I got my projects going on and stuff. I got a lot of fingers in a lot of pies. Unit 5 isn't even close to done yet and I still got my community service for the parking lot fight. Just go knock on some doors or something. It belongs to someone. It has to belong to someone. It's a baby."

I've watched Harley pull underwear out from the pool; I've found tiny T-shirts clogging the drains inside the bathrooms and spotted broken action figures with no heads standing in the windows on the second floor like damaged sentries.

"At four in the morning? You don't just have a baby wandering around and no one noticing, Harley. You don't just see that on a regular goddamn day. Where is the freaking phone?"

"Don't call the cops, man. We still gotta work stuff out with Lazlo and his friends. Look. We will figure it out. Just keep it here and I'll figure it out or whatever. You don't wanna do anything stupid anyway. You need to breathe. You need to leave it here with me. Go for a walk. The baby ain't yours anyway. How about I call Lazlo? He knows all the families in here. He's the one who brings 'em in here in the first place. I'll let his greasy face sort out this mess."

Eventually the frozen calf floated back to the surface; its body remained trapped under the ice. One eye stuck to the other side, staring up into the snow until we tried to clear off the pond for shinny. It stayed there throughout the winter months. We found other ponds, but sometimes stumbled back toward the calf without thinking. Its pupil seemed to swallow everything whole.

"Just give me the goddamn phone, Harley. Lazlo is a freak. I don't wanna deal with him."

You couldn't avoid its gaze.

"No."

I took Cheryl there after she told me about everything. I told her this is what happens sometimes. That sometimes we make mistakes. She told me I was stupid. Told me the calf only drowned because it was alone. People aren't alone, Cheryl said. People aren't ever alone like that. I asked her if the other cows would have pulled it out if they had the chance, asked if they would've made a chain together or fashioned a rope out of their tails. She just shook her head and turned back toward the house. I waited until she pulled out of the driveway in her Oldsmobile before following her footsteps through the snow. A few months later I heard from the hospital and left for the bus station with my hockey bag and three hundred bucks.

"It's a baby for Chrissakes. Just give me the goddamn phone, Harley. I'll meet them outside. Lazlo won't have to know about any of this—"

A weed whacker looks a lot bigger when it is swinging towards your face. Bits of wet grass hit my skin. I stumble back toward the wall and grab the lava lamp, tearing it free from its socket. Harley is shrieking something about rent control and fire code violations. I notice his pupils dilating as he fires up the weed whacker. It spits and coughs grey clouds into the air as he swings it across the room again. The lava lamp sails toward Harley's head and the baby starts wailing as I scoop it up into my arms. The calm flow of the liquid splatters across Harley's bearded face when the lamp shatters. I slam the office door behind me as he swings the whacker against the wall. I run toward the courtyard, screaming for some help, but my voice is hoarse and we all lock our doors in this place. The baby is soaked, a wet towel against my chest. The concrete slaps against my bare feet. I can hear women waking up and running showers in the dark. I can hear men pulling on boots and untying stubborn laces with their curses. Kids remain quiet in the darkness, waiting for some meagre sunlight to expose what it can inside this place.

The courtyard is empty and the pool is still. Small gnats drown slowly across its surface; they are drawn by the smell. The door clatters open behind me and the weed whacker shrieks as Harley bashes it against the concrete. They will tear this place down some day and find all the things we tried to hide inside the walls on Kingston Road. All the families smuggled on planes and booked in twin bed suites. With flashlights in the dark, they will find every one of us hiding behind ice machines and shower curtains, asking for a second chance, a bargain, a reprieve, a pardon for all the things eventually discovered between mattresses and deep down inside the drains. Harley tries to fire up his machine again; he screams that we all need to settle down for a second and I feel its wet wire nip at my back. The courtyard leads nowhere. All the windows I can see remain shut and blinded.

I jump into the pool.

The water is warm. I try to find the bottom with its endless coins, but I'm still holding the baby to my chest. I want to linger at the bottom, to wait out Harley until he gets tired or stoned again, but I can feel the baby shake against my ribs. Its lungs are too small; everything is too small. They found Harley's uncle floating here after Harley called the police. Lazlo said these things happen sometimes, happen to certain men. I know Harley can't bring his weed whacker into the water. The surface is glowing above us, but nothing kind waits up there.

There is a weight inside my hands and I can feel it beating. I push off the bottom of the pool with both feet, holding the little body above my head. I try not to think about the other little bodies inside this place, stashed here by men and women with numerous passports; all their files are sorted by date of birth. I don't know if Harley will wade into the water with his broken tools before someone calls the police. I don't know if anyone will call the police. I realize I don't know a lot of things, that I don't want to know a lot of things—I see only fragments from that elevator ride flickering on and off again. Water breaks above and chlorine burns my eyes.

The baby starts to shriek because it's not alone.

Acknowledgements

Thanks to all those who published these stories in earlier forms, including *Joyland*, *The Cleveland Review*, *Little Fiction*, *Drunken Boat*, *Burrow Press*, *Grain*, *The New Quarterly*, *Bluestem*, *The Good Men Project*, *Border Crossing*, *The Drum*, *Corium*, *Necessary Fiction*, *Metazen*, *The Rusty Toque*, *The Other Room*, *Monkeybicycle*, *Dr. Hurley's Snake Oil Cure* and *EVENT*.

Thanks to the Ontario Arts Council for supporting this project from the beginning. Thanks to Chris Bucci for finding something in my fiction.

Thanks to all my mentors, especially Miriam Toews for her incredible generosity and Jeff Parker for his sage advice.

Many thanks to everyone who helped inspire and improve these stories, especially Brendan Bowles, George Pakozdi, Suzannah Showler, Daniel Mittag, Troy Palmer and Karen Principato.

Special thanks to John K. Samson for believing in this book, and to Rick Wood and Kathleen Olmstead at ARP for bringing it to life. Major thanks to Leigh Ledare for the dogs.

Thanks to my family and my parents, Ed and Shelley. This book does not exist without you. You have always been there from the start.

And finally, thanks with love to Jen, who keeps the ship from sinking.

Andrew F. Sullivan is from Oshawa, Ontario, and graduated from the University of Toronto. He has worked in
a liquor warehouse and a video game store, and is the
associate fiction editor for *The Puritan*. Andrew's writing
has been been published in a number of literary journals,
including Grain, Joyland, and Little Fiction. *All We Want
is Everything* is his first book.